Reborn with Fire

The Telepathic Alliance Book III

Tanya M. Parr

iUniverse, Inc.
Bloomington

Reborn With Fire
The Telepathic Alliance Book III

iUniverse books may be ordered through booksellers or by contacting:

iUniverse
1663 Liberty Drive
Bloomington, IN 47403
www.iuniverse.com
1-800-Authors (1-800-288-4677)

ISBN: 978-1-4759-9286-1 (sc)
ISBN: 978-1-4759-9334-9 (ebk)

Library of Congress Control Number: 2013909655

Printed in the United States of America

iUniverse rev. date: 05/30/2013

PROLOGUE

Colt and Salis are sitting on her bed viewing Calidon's history tapes, when Thayer walks into the room without warning. They both jump up from the bed and stand facing Salis' now furious father.

"So this is why you've been refusing to spend hardly any time with me and your mother," Thayer says tightly, looking from one to the other. "You went behind our backs and did exactly what you wanted without any regards to my wishes."

Colt takes a protective stance in front of Salis. "You didn't really give us much of a choice Thayer. We tried . . ."

"I gave you the only choice that you needed Colton Blackwood." He says to him so sharply that Colt blinks in surprise. "There were reasons why I said you should wait. You should have understood from your training with Nightstorm that I would never deny anything without a good and valid reason."

Colt stands straighter at the mention of his training and his adoptive father. "That's true, but my adoptive father also would not have denied anything without first hearing why I wanted to do something and then weighing all of the information before deciding either way. He would have given his reasons for such a decision, and he also would have made sure that there was no chance of anyone suffering physically or mentally from his decision."

Thayer stiffens at the accusation that he would have caused suffering from his decision to give his daughter time to look at this relationship from a distance. He still does not see where the separation would cause either child to suffer unduly. "There is nothing that points to either of you suffering greatly by a short separation." He says standing firm on his decision. "So, until we reach Panthera, you Colt, will be confined to an isolation room and completely cut off from everyone. You young lady will stay in your room and speak only to your mother and me." He looks at each of them. "There will be no contact through the comm system either."

Colt blanches at this. "No Thayer! You can't do that! We need . . ."

"I can and I will young man! And at this point in time what you want or need is not high up on my priority list." Thayer tells him sharply, then stands aside, and nods at the two guards that have just arrived. "Please escort Mr. Blackwood to an Alpha room. He is to have no contact with anyone, especially the Princess." He nods again and the guards take Colt from the room. As they leave Thayer, notices that Colt refuses to fight the guards, sure that he knows that it would only make his and Salis' situation worse.

While being taken away, Colt hears, Salis cry out, "Father, no! Do not do this! We have to have some contact." Her voice fades as they step into the turbo lift and go down two decks to the holding rooms.

In Salis's cabin, she bursts into uncontrollable tears. When Thayer tries to comfort her, she pulls away from him. "Don't touch me! You've made it clear that what we want and need isn't important to you! Leave me alone!" She screams at him moving away from him and facing the wall trying to figure out what she and Colt could do to be together again. She did not know if she could handle not having any contact with him.

"It won't be that bad sweetheart, you'll see. When we get to Panthera . . ." He trails off as she turns to glare at him her face extremely pale.

"It will be that bad Father. We're supposed to be together and you won't let us. You won't listen to anything we have to say."

"You're too young to know that sweetheart. In time you'll see that . . ."

"In time I'll wish I were dead, or that you were. Go away father. I don't want to talk to you anymore. I don't want to see you right now. You won't listen to me, so why should I listen to you? You say that I'm too young to know something that affects my life and peace of mind. I think that you're too old and closed minded to realize that you don't know everything."

Thayer wonders if she knows that she is not making things any better. He realizes that she cannot help herself. That she is overly emotional, and therefore irrational. He sighs when she turns her back to him, lies down on the bed, and puts her face into her pillow.

Though he would like to upbraid her for speaking to him in such a manner, he realizes that she is upset and not thinking clearly. He's not sure what has gotten into her. Over the past several weeks, she has matured and come out of her shell. With a sigh, he finally leaves the room and returns to the lounge.

Without saying anything to the others in the room, he fixes himself a drink. After he finishes his first drink, he pours himself another and then turns to face his mate and the others. "I just found Colt in Salis' cabin." He tells them flatly, taking a large swallow of his drink.

"How was he able to stay hidden from us for so long? Surely Sarah would have sensed his extra life signs, especially if he's been keeping to Salis' cabin." Brockton Centori asks from his seat on one of the sofas.

The lounge is a large cabin area with several sitting areas, and a personal dining area near the portals. The area where Brockton and the others are sitting has several sofas and loveseats in a box formation with a square coffee table in the center.

"I'm not sure how he did it. I didn't bother to ask. All I knew was that they had defied me when I told them that he couldn't come with us." He admits, wondering himself why Sarah or Stephen hadn't picked up the extra life sign.

Leyla walks over to his side and looks up at him. "What did you do Thayer?"

"I separated them. I had Colt taken to an Alpha room. He's to have no contact with anyone. At least not until we reach Panthera. And Salis is to stay in her room with only you and me to talk with."

"Oh Thayer, was that really necessary?" Leyla asks shaking her head at such a punishment. Neither of the children would understand such harsh punishment. She didn't quite understand it herself. She had never even heard of cutting a child off from all contact.

He frowns down at his mate wondering why she wasn't agreeing with him on this. "Yes it was necessary Leyla. They will not be allowed to go against our wishes without receiving a punishment. I know that things have been rough this last year, but that's no excuse for defying their elders."

"Thayer, they may have felt that they had no other choice." Sheyome points out from her position near one of the windows. "You didn't really give them a chance to explain to you why they felt they needed to stay together. At home, I felt that their bond was very strong for ones so young. In fact it felt almost as strong as what an adult feels when they first come in contact with the one meant to be their mate."

"Yes, I noticed that as well." Trocon Damori adds. "It's quite unusual to see such a strong bond develop so quickly between two people, let alone children. It's almost as if they were meant to meet and bond."

Thayer sighs and takes a sip of his drink. "Even so, a three month separation wouldn't have killed either of them. The point is, they went against my wishes and now they are paying the price for doing so."

"But what price will you pay for your decision my love?" Leyla asks softly looking up at him. She sees the pain he is already suffering from his decision, but she has to make him think about what he's doing and what he's already done. "You have to consider the fact that you could be wrong no matter how right your decision feels. Not only that, but without knowing for sure how they would be affected, you have completely cut them off from each other. I think this may cost you more than you think."

Over the next day and a half, everyone on the ship learns what has happened and suffers from the anguished mental cries of the Princess.

Salis refuses to talk to anyone until Colt has returned to her side. She doesn't care if anyone thinks that she's acting like a baby and spoiled brat. Her whole body, mind, and soul are hurting. They feel like they're being torn apart, and her father wasn't doing anything to stop the pain. As time goes on, she begins to feel weaker and weaker. Her cries for Colt become weaker with each passing hour. Near the time of the noon meal, she stops calling for him and curls into a fetal position. She can no longer stand the pain and begins shutting down her mind to everything around her. She can see no point to going on when every movement and thought hurt unbearably.

Just after the noon meal, Thayer receives a message from his mother back on Manchon. 'Thayer, hear me and listen. Unless you wish to lose your daughter for all time, you will release Colt to go to her NOW! Salis cannot withstand the pain she's in much longer. Both of their lives may very well be at stake, including Merri's.'

Though he would like to ignore her, he knows that his mother would never interfere in such a personal problem without cause. Thayer is then forced to admit that Salis and Colt's bond is a lot stronger than he had believed, he had heard and seen what this separation was doing to them, though none of it really made any sense to him. His doubts also didn't justify his keeping them apart any longer. He has no wish to lose the daughter of his heart because of being too stubborn to admit when he's wrong, or that he doesn't know everything. Besides that, Salis' cries had tapered off over the last few hours and had stopped completely just before lunch, which has worried him even more.

Going to the room where Colt was being held, he is shocked to discover how weak Colt has become in the short time that he and Salis had been separated. He dismisses the guards and personally lets Colt out of the room before taking him to Salis' cabin. He has to nearly carry the boy to the cabin.

Colt forces himself to look up at Thayer, his throat too constricted to speak, so that he can touch his mind. 'We have to hurry Thayer. She's giving up. The pain is too much for her, and she doesn't want to feel it anymore.'

Thayer frowns as they hurry to Salis' room. When they enter the room, he can barely feel the faint stirring of her energy. Salis barely moves when they enter the room and Thayer notices that her color is very bad. He helps Colt over to the bed and lays him down beside her. When they finally come into physical contact on the bed, Thayer notices a soft rosy light engulfing them. After waiting several minutes, he starts to get concerned when neither one moves.

Just when he begins to think that he should call for medical help, Colt begins to stretch and then sits up slowly. Colt lightly caresses Salis's hair and talks softly to her. After a couple more minutes, she stirs and turns to look up at him. Realizing that he is real and that there is no longer any pain, she sits up with a glad cry and wraps her arms around his neck, holding him close and weeping on his shoulder.

"I'm sorry; I couldn't take it any more Colt. It hurt too much, and all I could think was that I had to get away from the pain. I didn't know what to do, how to make them understand." She tells him still weeping on his shoulder.

Clearing his throat, Thayer takes a step closer to the bed and looks down at his daughter. "Salis, I am so sorry. I honestly didn't believe that your bond to each other had grown so strong. Never have I heard of such a strong bond between young people. If I had known, I never would have separated you. Salis, I never wanted to hurt you, never wanted you to feel pain again. I only wanted for you to take the time to be sure that what you were feeling was real."

Once again, in her right mind, and seeing that her father has been suffering just as much as she and Colt have, Salis apologizes to him for the way she had behaved. "I never meant what I said about wishing you would die Daddy. My mind just couldn't cope with what was happening and I said the first thing that came into my head that would hurt you as much as we were hurting." Colt also apologizes for his words and actions.

"There's no need for either of you to apologize." Thayer assures them both. "It was my fault for not listening to you when you first came to me with your request. You were right Colt when you said that I didn't have all the facts before I made my decision. My only excuse is that I didn't want to believe that you were both growing up so fast. I wanted to keep you both as you were before you met." He grimaces in self-derision. "But that's no excuse either. You have the right to follow your destinies, and no one, not even a father or a king, has the right to interfere in such things. I also never should have cut you off from any contact."

For the rest of the trip Salis and Colt try to explain what has been happening to them to Thayer and Leyla. They want to understand what is and what will happen to them in the coming years.

"You'll have to talk to Kasmen when we get home. Neither one of us knows anything about what's happening to you. Even Trocon has never seen such a thing as happened with the two of you." Leyla tells them. She was glad that Royanna had contacted Thayer when she had otherwise they would have lost both of the children possibly even three, since she didn't know how Colt's death would affect his twin Merri. Sarah had been monitoring Salis during the separation and she had told them later that if they had waited an hour or two longer Salis would have slipped into a coma and then died. If that would have happened, she knew that Colt would have followed her.

When they reach Panthera, they stay with the Aquilians and Pantherians for nearly two weeks going over the agreement for the Alliance. Everything was agreed upon, including the young people's part in the Alliance. Before leaving, Leyla and Thayer invite the royal families to the christening of their unborn child. They leave assured that the Telepathic Alliance is well on its way to becoming all that they wish it to be, and all that it is supposed to be.

CHAPTER 1

FIVE YEARS LATER: 2802

For the past five years, Colton Blackwood has been Salis Starhawk's constant companion and one of her personal bodyguards. Whenever she has to make a tour of the planet, or make a public appearance, Colt and Sheyome are with her to ensure that she is never in danger.

While at the palace, they study hard to achieve a high position as junior ambassadors for the Alliance even though they have never gone to any of the other planets like most of the other young people. Because of Salis' position, it just isn't possible for her to participate in such a way, so she and Colt have been working and studying with the adults and young people that have come to Calidon. When not involved with palace business they study the different laws and customs of each of the Allied worlds trying to find common grounds in all. They have now been made Nauba junior ambassadors, the highest position before becoming an adult ambassador. Right now, they are going over the reasons for why the King and Queen should pick them to approach the people of Savôn, a planet of which was suspected of having telepaths. It would be their first actual personal involvement, and it would be their first time off Calidon since the Alliance was formed, without the entire royal house with them. The hardest part would be getting Leyla and Thayer to let go as parents rather than just as King and Queen.

"I think that we should be the ones chosen to go because we're young and we wouldn't make anyone feel threatened by our presence." Salis says to Colt as she arranges some flowers on a side table.

"True, and we're more open-minded than a lot of the older people up for the post. Where we look for the good before the bad, most of them look for the bad before searching out the good. We would also be representing the royal family of Calidon, not just the Alliance. I think that it would give more strength to any promises we have to make but I would rather not use that tie unless we absolutely had too. There would still be the possibility that they would not believe that we could hold such authority because of our young age though." He points out as he puts the finally touches on the picture he was painting for his sister Cassie.

"Yes, all of that is true, but we also have to have the power to make those promises." She points out looking up at him.

"We'd have that power. You use it every time we tour the planet or go out in public and someone asks you for something." Colt reminds her and then points out, "We wouldn't agree on important things without your parents okay first. I've noticed that a few of the older ambassadors that have been sent on missions like this have agreed to things that later the Alliance Council have had to either renegotiate or refuse completely. When that happens, it just puts a strain over everything. " Putting down his paintbrush, he steps back and studies his work. Not quite satisfied with the way it looks, he kinetically alters it here and there and then studies it again before nodding his approval.

Salis looks at the picture and nods her approval as well. "You forgot to sign it again." She smiles as she points to the lower right hand corner where his name should appear. Nearly every painting that he's done she's had to remind him to sign it.

Sighing, he kinetically signs the picture, then removes it from the easel, and sets it aside to dry. He looks up at the chronometer. "We meet with your parents in thirty minutes to find out their decision, and I still need to get cleaned up and changed."

"You're not going to wear your guard uniform are you?" She asks with a slight frown. "I think your Nauba uniform is definitely called for."

Colt frowns as he remembers the way the uniform fit him across the shoulders. "Well I guess, since this involves that position, we should both dress the part." He agrees still frowning. "Though I need to speak to the tailor about redoing the shirt and jacket again. They're still too tight against my wing blades. It always feels like they're being pushed out through my chest."

"Did you try refitting them yourself?" She asks with a frown of her own. They had had this same problem a few other times.

"Yes, but the tailor that made them, made them kinetically, so it's more difficult to alter the patterns." He tells her thinking of the one time he had tried to alter his shirt and jacket. By the time he was done, you couldn't tell what they were supposed to be.

"We'll stop by and talk to him about it after we speak to mother and father. If he can't do the work he was hired to do, knowing of your special needs, then we'll have to find someone else to do the job. There's no reason why you should have to go through this so many times. You better go and wash up and change." She pushes him towards his room and then goes to her own to change.

Thayer and Leyla go over the applications for the assignment of psi detection on Savôn one last time. Most of the applicants have been on such assignments before and have handled them if not perfectly, then adequately. The only ones not experienced with such work, and the youngest to ever even be considered for such an assignment with any real conviction for the position are Salis and Colt. Their passion for this assignment is stronger than any other that has applied for this or any of the previous assignments.

"They have some valid reasons for why they should be chosen for this." Thayer points out looking at his mate. "Besides, they really need the experience."

"I agree with all of that, but are they ready and able to make the necessary decisions without much input from us? You know that things can happen unexpectedly, and quick decisions will have to be made, are they ready to accept such responsibility?"

Thayer sets aside the files he's been looking over. Looking at his mate, he realizes that deep down she doesn't want to let Salis go yet. "We can't hold her back love. She's old enough to take on more responsibilities, they both are. It's not as if they haven't had responsibilities before. Salis does a tour every three months and she's handled each one very well. Her decisions were carefully considered and made to benefit all those concerned. I think that we should let them do this and see how they handle it. If we don't show faith in them now, they may not reach their full potential. They may even give up, and you know that Salis isn't in the position where she can give up her responsibilities. We have to have faith in her and show it if the people are to have faith in her as well."

Leyla frowns remembering in the past, he was the one with the doubts of sending them out and her doing the reassuring that they were ready for the responsibility. Her frown clears and she begins to laugh. Though they would be leaving the planet, it really was no different from what they did here on Calidon and it wasn't as though they would be alone.

"Alright. We'll let them handle this assignment and see what happens, but I want to take stronger safety precautions." She warns him. She may agree but she still wasn't going to take any chances with her oldest daughter around strangers. There would be no chance of the daughter of her heart not coming home in one piece.

Thayer nods and leans over to kiss her, then sits back and closes his eyes. 'Salis, you and Colt come to our meeting chamber for briefing on the Savôn assignment.'

When they arrive, Thayer can tell that both are trying to contain their excitement for being chosen for this mission. They listen carefully as he and Leyla go over everything that will need to be done.

They explain that Colt and Salis would need to see what the people of the planet felt about psi energy before doing anything, especially letting the people know why they are there. If the majority of the planet is against psi's, it would be best not to approach them on a planet wide scale, but to approach those with abilities on an individual or small group basis.

"We'll send two dozen others with you to help evaluate the planet. They will be under your command, and you will have to establish for yourselves that you are up to the position." Thayer tells them not willing to influence how their crew would respond to them. "They'll know that you're in command, but you'll have to prove yourselves to them. If for some reason there is any doubt, we are to be contacted to decide how to proceed."

"I think that it would be better if we went alone father. With that many people, we might draw the Federation's attention more to the planet. They've been watching us more closely for any new moves or activities, and we already know that they've had some contact with these people at one time or another."

Colt looks up from his notes. "Salis is right Thayer. With that many psi the Federation would know that we were up to something and come to investigate. Besides, you've never sent that many on any of the other missions." Colt points out evenly before continuing. "I'm surprised that they haven't already tried to get them to join the Federation. I know that we can handle everything on our own, and not draw too much attention. If they should show up we could cover ourselves by saying that Salis is on vacation or something like that."

"Even if you could handle everything Colt, you still need someone with you in case of an emergency or something going wrong." Leyla points out reasonably. "If you were to get cut off from the ship or lost your abilities for an unknown reason, someone would need to be there to help you out."

"She's right. No matter how important this assignment is, your safety, both of you, comes first." Thayer tells them standing near the fireplace. "If you insist on doing this alone then I think that for safeties sake, we should send Stephen with you. He can monitor you both and analyze any data you come up with."

Salis and Colt look at each other for several seconds which Thayer and Leyla know means that they are speaking privately to each other on this new plan and the addition of the android.

'Your parents are right love. It would be best if we had someone with us just in case.'

'But we'll have to make sure that Stephen understands that he can only act if we call on him. He has to allow us to try and get out of any situations on our own first.'

'Well, we can program him for that. So do we agree to their terms?'

'Yes, we agree.'

"Is there anything else we will have to agree to?" Colt asks before giving their agreement.

"Yes." Leyla says looking at each of them and knowing that this would be the hardest part for them to agree to. "Sarah's box on your cruiser is to be activated as an extra precaution, not only for your safety, but for the safety of the ship as well."

Salis sighs knowing that she should have expected such a request. Every Calidonian ship made had a similar box installed for Alliance safety, whether it got used or not was generally left up to the captain. "All right mother, but you have to make her understand that she has to follow our orders and not tell us what to do or how to do it. She's always trying to take control no matter who's in charge."

Leyla grins and then quickly covers it. "I'll make sure that she understands, but you have to understand too, that neither she nor Stephen will allow either of you to put yourselves in known danger." She reminds them. It's a basic program that can't be over written. Her own father had written the program and put in safe guards that would prevent it from being altered in any way.

"I understand that mother. We don't plan on doing anything of the kind."

"Then everything is set." Thayer says walking back over to the table. "As soon as your ship is ready you can leave for Savôn. I suggest that you take along some extra equipment for any mechanical problems that might arise. Just remember that it should only take a month to get all the information needed and make a decision. If for whatever reason you should decide that they would not make a good addition to the Alliance, contact us first and let us go over everything. If it becomes necessary, and there are more normal then psi, we may decide to offer the psi population the option of moving to one of the Alliance worlds or staying on Savôn. We would also ask that they not use their abilities to the determent of others if they decide to stay on their home world."

The papers are signed, and placed in a special computer box that will place the information into the main computer system. As they discuss how long it should take to complete the each aspect of the assignment, Christa Starhawk bursts into the room followed closely by Kota Centori, arguing with each other the whole time.

"Did not do it 'Ota. Sula did 'cause she wasn't watching." Christa stops at her sister's side and leans against her.

"She wasn't watching because you distracted her. If you're not going to play fair, then you shouldn't play at all." Kota tells her stopping beside Leyla.

"I was playing fair. She . . ."

"Hold on. What's going on here?" Leyla asks looking from her daughter to Kota. "Did something happen to Sula Nese?"

"Uh-huh. Christa made her fall off the beam and she hurt her arm." Kota tells her with a slight glare at Christa.

"Did not. She wasn't watching what she was doing and tripped over the apan that landed on the beam. If she was watching she wouldn't have tripped." Christa protests to her mother, then looks at Kota, and accuses, "She was messing with you instead of playing the game and following the rules like she was 'pose to. She glares at Kota never backing down and he glares back.

Salis looks down at her sister. 'Did you call the apan Ista?' She asks knowing that sometimes her sister called the birds to her. She could talk to almost any animal on the planet, and they talked to her in return and they all understood each other.

Christa looks up at Salis. 'No Lissa. I tried to make him move. He came to tell me that his mate hatched four babies. I tried to tell Sula he was there, but she ignored me.'

'How did you try to make him move?' Salis asks her knowing that her sister had to have done something desperate to try to save the bird especially if the other girl had ignored a warning.

'I . . . I moved . . . I moved the beam.' Christa's eyes get big with the realization of what she had done. 'I did make Sula fall. I didn't mean to Lissa. She was going to step on him cause she wasn't watching. He didn't know he was in danger.'

Salis puts her arm around Christa's shoulders. "I understand sweeting." Salis looks over at Kota. "Was Sula messing around with you instead of paying attention to what she was doing Kota? Instead of paying attention to her surroundings and what was going on around her?"

Kota looks down at his shoes and then shrugs his shoulders. "I guess so Lissa."

"Did you see the apan land on the beam Kota?" Leyla asks him tipping his face up so that he has to look at her. When he shrugs, again, she frowns slightly at him and she takes that to mean that he had seen the bird land on the beam. "Did you warn Sula that it was there?" He shakes his head. "Then why did you accuse Christa of not playing fair? She was trying to protect the apan because Sula wasn't paying attention to what she was doing. Just from what little I've heard you and Sula are the ones being unfair."

Kota considers that for a minute and then, "I'm sorry Christa." He says quietly not really looking at her, but meaning his apology. He didn't know why he hadn't warned Sula about the apan. He had heard Christa say something to her and he had seen it himself, but hadn't added his warning, which might have prevented the accident from happening.

For several seconds Christa just looks at him unsure if she should forgive him for what he had said to her earlier, or that he had chosen Sula over her, and then she sighs. She couldn't really stay mad at him. He was her best friend and she knew that he loved her. "It's okay Kota. I guess I could have done something else to make the apan move, but she almost stepped on him and he wouldn't have known it was coming. He just became a daddy. I didn't mean for her to get hurt, but she wouldn't listen to me when I warned her he was there."

Leyla closes her eyes as she feels Sula's mother Phala linking with her about Sula. After listening carefully, she tells her about the apan and Christa's attempt to save it from harm. She also tells her about Sula not obeying the rules set down for the children using the beam. Phala tells her that she thought there was something more to it than what Sula had told her because of the feelings of guilt coming from her daughter. They both agree that all three of the children would be equally punished for their parts in the incident.

Leyla opens her eyes and looks at each of them. "Sula cracked her forearm when she fell." She tells them and then goes on quickly when Christa gasps and turns as white as a cloud. "It's all right sweetheart. Rachael healed the crack and Sula's arm is fine."

Christa bursts into tears and collapses into her sister's arms. "I didn't mean for her to break anything. I promise mommy, I didn't mean it to happen."

"We know you didn't mean for it to happen sweeting. It was an accident, but from now on, you're going to have to be more careful. Though all life is precious, sometimes we have to choose a human life over an animal no matter how much it may hurt us." Salis tells her softly. "It's not easy, but sometimes it's necessary. Do you understand? You feel bad because Sula broke her arm, but you would be feeling worse if she had hurt her head or her back when she fell. Either one of those injuries could have been fatal."

"Salis! There's no need for that." Leyla admonishes her oldest daughter, seeing Christa go even paler.

"Yes, there is Mother. She has to know what could have happened from her actions, and I've always promised her that I would tell her the whole truth no matter how bad it might be," Salis says, looking at her mother and then back at her sister. "Do you understand now why we have to think of people first? Yes, it would have been sad if the apan had died, but it would have been worse if Sula had been. All life is precious, but we have to think of how each loss will affect not just one but many."

Christa sniffles and nods her head. She understood everything her sister was telling her, even though she didn't like it, she knew that a human life had to come first. She looks at her mother with regret in her eyes. "Can I go and tell Sula that I'm sorry mommy? I want her to know that I didn't do it on purpose, that it really was an accident. I would never choose an animal over a person."

"Of course you wouldn't sweetheart; you can go and talk to her." Leyla agrees. As Christa and Kota walk to the door, she calls out to them. "For one week none of you will be allowed playtime. When you're not in school, you will go to the center and help with whatever needs to be done there. Is that clear?" Both children nod their heads and then leave the room quietly. Salis and Colt stand to leave as well.

"Do you think she'll be all right mother? I wasn't trying to be hard on her; I just wanted her to understand what could have happened. She needs to realize that there can be strong negatives to the things we do even if we're trying to do something good. She didn't think of all of the consequences of what she was doing." Salis says looking at the door in concern for her baby sister. Christa was a smart child, but a lot of the time she let her emotions control her and didn't think things through. She had been like that since the day she was born. It didn't help that Kota was at the center of the incident today. I hope that she would realize what was happening and find it in herself to control her jealousy. Kota would always have female friends, but Christa was the one he cared for.

"I'm sure that she will honey. As you said, I think that she needed to hear what could have happened. It hurt her, but now she'll start considering what might happen when she does something. I don't think anything like this will happen again with her or with Kota. He let Sula flirt with him because he wanted to see what Christa would do. He feels badly now because Sula was hurt when he could have prevented it. I don't think he'll allow anyone to come to harm again because of something he did or didn't do." Leyla assures her.

"I think that he's learning that it's not right to tease the people you care about in certain ways either." Colt says as he and Salis walk out of the room. "He's confused about what he's feeling and unsure of how to handle it because she's younger than him and he's unsure of how Christa feels about him. He knows she loves him, but I don't think he realizes that it's the same for her. They'll find the way one of these days."

Salis nods and frowns slightly. "I just hope that Father doesn't realize what's going on between them. They're even younger then we were. If he even suspected that they were developing a bond like ours, he would have the priests and Grandmother Rachael working on a way to weaken the connection, if not sever it completely."

Colt frowns himself. "I don't think that he would take it that far. He learned from our experience that you couldn't control fate. Besides, I don't think that their bond can ever be broken. If anything, he'll try to help them through it."

Covering her eyes with her hands, Salis groans. Thinking of her father attempting to help anyone through a bonding was not something that she really wanted to consider. "How embarrassing. I hope that doesn't happen either."

"We'll have to wait and see won't we." Colt wraps an arm around her shoulders and they continue on to their suite of rooms. They would tell Sheyome of their appointment after they celebrate in private.

Over the next three days, they pack and get their ship ready for the trip. Salis makes sure that Sarah and Stephen have all the information available on Savôn. They carefully go over their list of things they need to take and double-check everything. Stephen double checks all of the electronics equipment and replaces any components that are running slower then he thinks they should. Sarah goes over all of her navigational charts and systems, plotting their course to keep them from any areas run by the Federation. She would make sure that her charges were as safe as possible.

CHAPTER 2

After preparing their ship for their journey and saying good-bye to their friends, Salis and Colt climb aboard and begin the trip to Savôn. They stay on the bridge and watch Calidon become just another distant star before letting Sarah take control of the ship. That was one of the upsides of having Sarah's unit on the ship. It gave them the time to do what they need to do to get ready for their mission without worrying about piloting the ship, and Sarah was better than autopilot because she didn't need their input for anything.

"I think I'll go and unpack now Colt." Salis says as they leave the bridge. "Mother insisted that I bring a couple of formal outfits, just in case. If I don't want them to be permanently wrinkled, I need to get them hung up."

Colt nods and watches her walk down the corridor. When she turns the corner, he turns to find Stephen looking at him. Not saying anything, he walks to the nutrition center and fixes himself a cup of herbal tea. Stephen follows and waits until he is sitting, before speaking.

"She's not sure of this assignment." He makes it a statement instead of a question.

"It's not the assignment she's not sure of Stephen, but herself." Colt sighs and sips at his tea. "She's beginning to doubt that she's really ready for something like this, that she knows enough to be of benefit to all those concerned. First contact is very nerve racking when it's your first time."

"If she wasn't ready, neither Leyla or Thayer would have agreed to let you both do this on your own no matter how compelling your argument." Stephen points out logically.

Colt looks at him and then down into his tea. "I know. The problem is we should have volunteered earlier to go on other assignments as observers. It would have given her a chance to see what others did and how they handled different situations. Watching holograms of other assignments doesn't really give you a feel for what's taking place." He finishes the tea and pushes the mug away. "The things she dealt with at home are minor compared to what we may come up against on Savôn. Any number of things could go wrong, and she's worried that she's going to make mistakes that Leyla and Thayer are going to have to fix."

"Do you think that she can handle it?" Stephen wants to know.

"Yeah, I think she can do it. She's a lot stronger then she sees herself, and she proved herself five years ago when she helped make some pretty serious decisions that have played a major part in the Alliance." He reminds the android. "Leyla and Thayer have included her in making decisions that will and have affected a lot of people's lives over the years and those to come. Now all of these people are very happy and living normal lives again. I have no doubt that she can handle anything we have to deal with so that it will be fair to all of those involved."

Stephen nods and turns to the door as Salis enters. "We need to go over what measures you and Sarah need to take in case we run into trouble on Savôn Stephen."

"Of course Salis. Shall we go into the lounge where you'll both be more comfortable?"

She nods and leads the way to the lounge. As they go she, studies the color scheme of the ship's interior. Though the off-white walls are practical, it appears very dull to her senses. She remembers the bright interesting colors done throughout Altia Siberi's family cruiser. Altia's maternal great-grandfather had insisted that if they must travel through the darkness of space, then they should at least have some color to look at. Her mother Tacia and her aunt Laica had then done the ship's interior in soft pastels from the walls to the furnishings. They were all colors associated with the family. Salis wonders if she should ask Sarah to add some color to the walls. It would certainly make the ship more cheerful and less boring for the time she and Colt would be onboard.

As they enter the lounge, she decides that she would go ahead and have Sarah add some color throughout the ship. After all, they had to be comfortable and relaxed for this assignment didn't they? Moreover, she was far from relaxed.

Their discussion starts with the different safety procedures that they could use in case of an emergency. After they've rejected several for one reason or another, Sarah mentions that they could implant locators. Salis objects to this, telling them that the locators range would not be strong enough should they go more than ten miles from the ship.

"That's no longer true Salis. We have developed a new locator that has a much broader range." Sarah assures her. "With this new unit, I can track you to anywhere on the planet surface or below ground. Be it a few feet or five hundred miles, I could find you."

"And if we were five hundred miles away then something would definitely be wrong." Salis snaps. "Why should we go that distance from our ship on a planet we know very little about?"

"I did not say that you would, but if you did, we could still track you and transport you back to the ship if necessary."

"We could transport ourselves Sarah if it came to that. It wouldn't be necessary . . ."

"It might be Salis." Colt interrupts her. "You just said yourself that we know very little about the planet. That goes for the people as well. For all we know they could have something capable of blocking psi abilities. What would we do then? At least with the locators it would be easier for them to find us for transport. They wouldn't have to worry about getting the wrong people."

Salis frowns at him and then gets up to pace around the lounge. She knows that they're both right, and that it's a good safety measure, but she doesn't like the idea of an implant. It would give Sarah too much freedom to pull them out if she thought that they were in a situation they couldn't handle.

"All right. If I agree to this, it would only be under the condition that neither you or Stephen could decide if we were in danger. That decision must be ours and ours alone. The only times you would be able to take action would be if we asked for it, or our biorhythms were so low that you knew that we were incapable of ordering such an action."

"And at what level do you consider low enough for us to take action?" Sarah asks stiffly not liking such limitations to her primary protocols.

Salis turns to look at Colt and Stephen. Neither of them offers any suggestions and she looks away. A good biorhythm ran at about seventy-five when normal, and anything below that showed signs of different stages of lower consciousness. A gradual decline to fifty is associated with the beginnings of a normal sleep and usually stops at forty when the person is fully a sleep. However, when unconsciousness is forced, it can go as low as twenty-five or fifteen in a matter of a few seconds. "If it gets to forty-five and we haven't contacted you, or it goes down quickly to say twenty-five or lower, then you can take action on your own."

"At that forty-five you're nearly into a full sleep Salis."

"Yes, I know which wouldn't be normal since we plan to stay on the ship while we're on the planet. If it drops lower, you'll know that we're in trouble. Anything else, we should be able to handle ourselves. With any luck, none of these things will be necessary." Salis says returning to her seat next to Colt. She's not sure if she's trying to convince them or herself that they could handle anything that doesn't knock them out.

"Since we won't arrive at Savôn for another two and a half weeks, we'll wait until the week we are to arrive before placing the implants." Stephen informs them standing and looking down at them. "If you will now excuse me, I will go and prepare you a meal." They both nod and watch him leave.

Colt turns back to Salis. "Why did you object so vehemently to the idea of the implants? It was the best suggestion that could be thought of for what we need."

Salis looks down at her hands and sighs. "It wasn't because I didn't think it was a good idea, just that I didn't want Sarah to be able to be in a position to take decisions out of our hands." She explains looking up at him. "She has the tendency of taking over lately whenever I'm trying to do something that even has a suggestion of danger. When she thinks I'm making a wrong decision she butts in. I don't want her doing that on this assignment. If something does go wrong, I want to know that I did everything possible to correct it, especially if it's my fault that it went wrong."

"Then why don't you just explain that to her? I'm sure that if you did she would understand and try to restrain herself from interfering." He says confidently, though he has some doubts. He knew that many of Sarah's actions were because she cared deeply for Salis.

Salis laughs a little and then moves closer to his side and leans her head against his shoulder. "The day Sarah learns restraint, I'll come up with a body for her to become completely self-mobile. She won't have to be carried around by anyone and will be able to do everything that Stephen does."

"I will hold you to that Salis Starhawk. I've got it all on tape, so that you can't back out." Sarah puts in and then waits a few seconds before telling them, "Stephen has your food ready."

"Thank you Sarah. Please tell him that we'll be there in a few minutes." Colt says looking at Salis' face. She closes her mouth and glares at him. He can't understand why she didn't think about the fact that Sarah would still be listening. Before she can say anything that could cause a huge argument, he kisses her until she collapses against him. Releasing her lips, he looks down at her and smiles. "Now let's go and eat before it gets cold." He stands up and then pulls her up beside him, and leading her to the galley where Stephen serves them and then goes to study the information on Savôn once more. They eat in silence for several minutes and then Salis looks up at Colt.

"I guess I shouldn't have been surprised that she was listening." Salis admits and then louder, "She still doesn't know when to give people any privacy." They hear a grumble and then a click as Sarah turns off her audio system to the galley. Colt and Salis laugh and then finish their meal. After cleaning up the center, they head back to the lounge to relax. Colt begins a painting of the palace to send back to Aeneka on Earth. Salis was going to take it to Manchon and then send it with the weekly visitors to her maternal grandmother when she goes to study under Royanna.

Salis sits at the writing desk to write in her journal about what has happened so far on their journey. Her argument with Sarah, and the deal that had been unintentionally agreed to with the computer unit. She puts down that if Sarah can keep her side of the deal,

Salis would find a way to make an android body for Sarah to become mobile. Putting down her journal, she looks at Colt and wonders why her mother or grandfather Saitun hadn't already designed a body for Sarah. After all, she had been in the Katmen family service for over forty years. It shouldn't be too hard to come up with something. They could have even gotten her a shell and downloaded Sarah's memories into it. The only difference between her and Stephen would be strength. She would still be stronger than any human would, but they would have to keep her a little weaker then Stephen. He was the only one that could really control her on any level, and they needed to keep it that way.

Suddenly, without any warning, both Colt and Salis stop what they're doing and clutch at their heads. Colt sets down his paintbrush and looks at Salis. "You felt it too?"

"Yeah. It was so strange. Like a tingling going through my mind. I've never felt anything like it before."

"Me neither. Maybe we should have the med unit check us over. It may be some kind of space sickness." Colt suggests walking over to stand in front of her.

Salis frowns doubting that it was something like that, but nods and then stands to follow him to the medical center. While Colt programs the unit, Salis strips down to her undergarments and then climbs inside the unit and pulls the lid down. Within ten minutes they're both done and waiting for a diagnosis. When the unit tells them that they are in perfect health and it can find no deviation in their normal patterns, they frown at each other.

"Sarah, is the med unit functioning correctly?" Colt asks still frowning knowing that something was wrong with them.

"Yes it is Colt. You are both in excellent physical and mental health." She assures him.

"Then what is causing the tingling in our minds Sarah? It hit us both at the same time about twenty minutes ago." Salis tells her in a puzzled voice.

"Since there is no medical reason for the sensation, I would have to say that you are probably showing an early sign of the lifemating burn. It means that soon you will begin to feel the burning associated with having found your lifemate, and that your lifemating is near at hand. Though I believe that you still have a few years before you must complete the mating."

"But we're too young to start the burning Sarah. Rachael and father said if we were meant to be lifemates the burning wouldn't start for at least another three years or so."

"I'm sorry Salis, but that is the only explanation that I can come up with."

"All right Sarah. Thank you." She says softly looking at Colt. When she hears the audio click off she sighs. "Now what do we do? I don't know about you, but I'm not really ready to become lifemated."

Colt frowns slightly and then shakes his head. "I'm not ready for it either, but we may not have any choice, though she did say that it could still take a few years. But you know as well as I do that once the burning starts, we have to go where it leads us or we could do ourselves harm both physically and mentally."

She notices that he's still frowning and steps closer to him. Looking into his eyes she reaches up, places her hand against his cheek, and realizes that her words had hurt him. "It's not that I don't want to be your lifemate Colt. I do. I love you more than I ever thought possible to love anyone but my family. However, right now I don't think that I'm old enough to deal with the responsibility and commitment that comes with a lifemating. Can you honestly say that you are?"

He continues to stare into her eyes, and realizes that he's not ready for that type of responsibility and commitment either. He wasn't sure if he was ready to share all that he was with her just yet. In some ways he still felt immature when it came to his feelings for Salis. He loves her deeply, and doesn't want to lose her, but is it enough to get them through the lifemating. He knows that if they aren't ready it could be just as dangerous to go through a lifemating, as it would be not to. "I know that you love me Salis. I love you too. You're right; neither of us is ready for a lifemating's responsibility. I think that when we get back home, we should check with Lord Metros and if nothing else have him put a mating shield around us to keep it in a manageable or dormant stage until we're both ready."

She nods and then sighs, dropping her hand to his chest. "I hope he can and that it works. Remember he tried it with Toleco Golese and Corma Sparra. It only lasted two months, and when it ended, they were in a lot of pain. They had to be lifemated within hours."

Reaching down, he lifts her chin so that she's looking him in the eye. "They were farther into the burning then we are, if we are. As long as we don't go past this tingle, to whatever is next, we should be all right." He lifts his brow to see if she agrees and she nods and then smiles slightly at him. "All right then. What do you say we turn in and get an early start in the morning?"

"Okay. I am kind of tired." She gives him a quick hug and then heads for the door. "I need to go and get my journal from the lounge. I'll see you in the morning."

Colt watches her rush from the room and then releases a soft sigh and begins straightening up the med center. When he's finished, he goes to the bridge to check on their course and speed and to ask Sarah to waken him early, then wishes her goodnight and goes to bed.

After retrieving her journal, Salis hurries to her room. In her room, she reaches out to her sister Christa. She wants to tell her what Sarah has said about the lifemating and to see if she agrees with her.

'I know you're not that old Ista, but you've listened and heard Grandmother Rachael talking and you know things that a lot of adults don't. Do you think that we're beginning the lifemating burn?' She asks quietly.

'That's what it sounds like Lissa. Do you want me to ask momma just to be sure?'

'No. I don't want her or father to start worrying. They might call us back home.'

'You should be okay till you come home Lissa. The tingle usually lasts a long time.'

'Yeah, that's what Colt thinks. I guess I just needed someone else to say tell me that too. Well, goodnight Ista. Sleep well little sister.'

'You too Lissa. I love you.' Christa says with a yawn in her thoughts.

'I love you too little one.'

Salis opens her eyes and smiles. Though others still treat her like a small child, and she sometimes acts like one, Christa is more intelligent than most adults. Grandmother Rachael says that Christa is the Great Ones blessing to mother and father, and that she will bring great comfort and strength to those she truly cares for. When she was born, her brain was more like an adults then a newborn babe. Salis agreed with her in this, because already her baby sister had given her the strength and courage to go beyond all that she thought was holding her back in her life, and answers to questions that the adults in their lives hadn't been able to answer. Undressing, she climbs into bed and relaxes into sleep. She knows that the Great One would guide her and Colt to their lifemating when it was their time, and in a way that they would need not fear when it did finally come.

A week later Stephen implants the locator chips behind their right ears. After they're in place, he tests the frequency to make sure that it doesn't bother either of them. He has to adjust Colt's to a lower frequency when the original causes him a severe headache.

Sarah adjusts her sensors to Colt's lower frequency and strengthens its output to maximize her intake of the signal. She wouldn't take any chances of losing his signal even for a short time.

Next Stephen gives them facial comm units. The listening device is placed just below the outer ear canal, and the transmitter is placed at the corner of the mouth. The unit can be activated with a mere flick of the tongue to the inside of the cheek under the transmitter. The listening unit causes a slight irritation for a short time until they get used to it.

Salis and Colt practice with the units until they can activate them with little or no thought. The units blend in with their skin tone and are so light that both of them forget that they even have them on.

When they are within a few days of reaching Savôn, Sarah taps into their computer system and gathers the information that Salis and Colt will need to learn something of the Savônian customs and cultures. They needed to be as prepared as possible when they make first contact.

For the next couple of days Colt and Salis go over everything that Sarah had gathered. They commit everything to memory and hope that they haven't missed anything that will cause them to make any social mistakes.

CHAPTER 3

When they reach Savôn air space, Sarah does a scan of the area and detects some strange energy readings from the planet's surface that she's never seen before. She runs through her files several times with no luck in tracing the energy type or use. Before taking the ship down, she warns Colt and Salis of these readings and that they should be extra careful until she and Stephen can identify the source and any dangers it might pose them.

"The configuration is unusual, but if we can separate it's components, we should be able to tell what it's use is."

"Is it anything that could cause us physical harm?" Colt asks wondering if they should put on environmental suits.

"No, there's nothing to indicate that it will harm you physically. Though the readings are high, it's dispersed over the whole planet and appears rather weak." She assures him. It was a puzzle that she didn't like. Something in her circuits was telling her that she should know what this was.

"Where will we be landing Sarah?" Salis asks looking at the scanner showing the northern hemisphere. "It would be easier if we knew where the planets leadership was located. Right now we're pretty much landing blind, with no idea who to talk with."

"We'll land in an area that has the largest population." Sarah tells her, lights up the area on the scanner, and then produces a holographic image of the city. "From the buildings and location, I would say that this is the most probable location for the seat of power on the planet. All of the other sites are smaller and less populated according to my readings."

"Is there a spaceport for us to land at?" Colt asks as he studies the hologram. "This area here." He points to an open area in the middle of the city. "It looks like it could be one. It's close to the middle of the city and there appears to be fewer buildings around it."

Sarah studies the area that he had indicated. "Yes, there appear to be several different types of air and space craft there. It will also be the best place to observe the city and possible to tap into their computer system if necessary. It's central location will work to our advantage."

"All right, go ahead and contact them and get permission for us to land. If they ask, tell them we are traveling around looking for planets that will accept tourism from other worlds on a regular basis. Compensation will be high on the worlds that agree." Colt tells her sticking to their plan to cover themselves should the Federation show up.

While Sarah is doing that, Stephen has the replicator make clothes for them to wear on the planet. By the time they're dressed Sarah has received permission for them to land. "You'll be met by the local district leaders and shown around before being allowed to go out on your own."

"Thank you Sarah. Please take us down."

Sarah takes them down and sets the ship close to the communications tower. Salis and Colt wait until the meeting party approaches the ship before opening the door. They walk out at a normal pace and stop at the end of the ramp. As the leaders approach, Colt sizes them up: They have two guards with them carrying side arms.

The leaders stop a couple of feet in front of them and then one steps forward holding out his hand to Colt. "Welcome to Savôn Mr. Wood. I am district head Adio Sette and these are my associates."

Colt shakes the older man's hand and nods to the others, not missing that the other two men's names were not given. "Thank you for allowing this visit Mr. Sette. This is my companion Miss Black." He introduces Salis and watches as the others barely acknowledge her presence. "Miss Black will be the one to decide if Savôn is acceptable as a vacation planet for our people gentlemen." Though they knew that women did not hold any positions of authority on the planet, they had decided to stay with Salis being the leader of this assignment.

The men look at each other and then at Salis. Sette extends his hand to her. "Welcome Miss Black. We're pleased that you are considering our home as a place for your people to vacation."

Salis shakes his hand briefly and nods. "Thank you Mr. Sette. I'm sure that it will not be a hard decision," she smiles slightly as he frowns, "but your planet is very beautiful and appears very restful."

The frown leaves his face and he begins to nod enthusiastically. "Yes, it is both." He indicates for them to follow.

As soon as Salis and Colt step off the ramp it retracts back into the ship and the door closes. The two guards stare for several seconds before turning away and following the group. They would be sure to report that it appeared the two that met with the district head were not the only ones on the ship.

Sette leads them to a large open-air car. Salis and Colt climb in first followed by Sette and then the others. The two guards climb into a further back seat and soon they are on their way into the city and away from the spaceport.

"Our planet is a peaceful place. For the past hundred and fifty years or so, we have been lucky enough to almost totally eliminate any and all criminal behavior. Though there is still some crime, it is mostly minor, non-threatening, and quickly taken care of. The people have been encouraged to report any activity that they feel is detrimental to the community as a whole, no matter how small, or who did the crime."

"So family reports on family, friend on friend, neighbor on neighbor." Colt states frowning slightly. "I would think that such actions would cause ill feelings amongst the people."

"At first it did, but now the people realize that when they report a petty theft, invasion of privacy," Sette shrugs his shoulders, "or any other crime against another, they are only helping those that need it. Those being reported realize that they are in need of help and soon thank the person who reported them to the proper authority."

As she listens, Salis frowns deeply. She did not like what she was hearing. This worlds government was using it's people to spy on each other and report any small infractions. How many of the people had abused the power they had been given. "I think that it would be a good idea Mr. Sette, if we were given a list of your laws and the things that your people consider criminal activities. I wouldn't want my people to unwittingly break a law or commit a crime."

"Of course Miss Black. I'll have one of my aides get a copy to you by tomorrow morning." Sette agrees.

For the next several hours, Sette and his associates describe the city and point out the points of interest. There are several holographic museums, a number of interactive theaters and movie houses, and quite a few riding stables, which have both live equine type horses and robotic. At the end of the tour, Sette suggests that they take them to one of the hotels, but Colt politely refuses.

"Though we appreciate the offer. We will be staying on our ship while we're here. As we compile information we need to enter that information quickly into our computer so that it can do a continuing compatibility study."

"I see. Well then, we'll return you to your ship. Would you care to join me and my wife for the evening meal?"

"Thank you that would be nice." Salis smiles at him hoping that he will not notice that it is forced. "When should we be ready?"

"It's three now." He says looking at his wrist unit. "I'll send a car for you in say five hours?"

"That will be fine." She agrees.

For the trip back to the ship, Salis lets Colt handle the conversation while she continues to study the people they are passing. Throughout the tour, both she and Colt had probed different individuals, trying to find any psi energy. Though they felt some energy, it was all too weak to locate any sources. Salis had also noticed that some of the people were wearing silver collars. The collars remind her of the ones that had been used on Calidon's penal moon until her parents had become the rulers of Calidon. The ones on Calidon were used to block psi abilities and she is beginning to wonder if that is what they are being used for here.

'We need to find out about these collars Colt. They remind me of the ones they used to use on our penal moon.'

'Do you want to ask Sette about them before he drops us off?' He asks turning to look at her with a raised brow.

'No, not right now. I doubt that he would give us a straight answer. It seems to me that they are picking and choosing what they tell us. Let's wait until later. Maybe we can get someone else to tell us.'

'All right. I'm going to find out if they'll let us walk around the port and city on our own. If there are any psi on this planet, the port will have to be able to handle the large cruisers.'

'Okay, that sounds like a good idea. Though I wish, we didn't have to, I think that we should start scanning their public minds and see what we can find out that Sette and the others aren't telling us. Besides the fact that women don't hold any high positions and are regarded as untrustworthy in matters of business.'

'How do you . . . ?'

'I touched his public mind when he shook my hand. Even though we already knew it from the information Sarah gathered for us to study.'

"Would you mind if we walk around the port and the city for a while? We would like to get a feel of everything and maybe ask a few questions here and there."

The car pulls to a stop near the communications tower. "I don't see that it would be a problem Mr. Wood." Sette agrees and hands Colt two gold badges. "These will allow you both to go anywhere on the planet except for restricted areas of course. It will also let our people know that they can freely answer your questions. Just realize that they won't answer any questions that would be considered a danger to world security." He warns them.

"That will be fine. I doubt very much if any of our questions would touch an area involving your world's security. If for some reason we should need any information of that type, we would of course be sure to contact the proper people in the proper manner." Salis assures him as they step out of the vehicle. She thinks to herself that they may be young but not stupid.

"Good, then I will see you both later this evening for the evening meal. Enjoy your afternoon." Sette nods to them and then taps the driver on the shoulder to signal him to drive on.

Salis and Colt watch the hover car disappear into the city and then turn to the tower. For the next hour they tour the facility and ask questions about worldwide communications and if their people would need any special clearances or not. Satisfied that they have covered their story of looking for a vacation planet they return to the ship.

As they approach the ship, the ramp comes down and the hatch opens. They enter and close the hatch behind them before going to the comm center. "Sarah, do you have anything on file about the collars we saw. They're silver in color and slightly resemble the ones used on the penal moon before Mother and Father came."

"There's no record of them in the files that I originally retrieved. I'll go through them again to make sure, and then ask their system about them. With the proper coding I should be able to get all the information we need."

"Do what you can Sarah. We're going to go out again and see if we can't locate that energy source. We'll be back in a couple of hours to get ready to go to dinner at Sette's at eight. Give us a reminder call at about six."

"All right Salis. Why don't you see if you can get one of the collars for Stephen to do an analysis on? It might help us." The computer suggests.

After changing into less conspicuous clothing, they go to Stephen's lab and get two of the small energy meters. Before leaving the ship, they put up mental shields to prevent any mind probes by other telepaths or by mechanical means. Once they leave the ship, they quickly walk to the nearest alleyway once they're sure that their mind shields are working. Once in the alley and sure that it's safe, they drop the shields that would protect them from mechanical probes, but keep in place the shield that would prevent another psi from reading their minds. They slowly move out into the street and look around before deciding which way to go.

They walk around talking to the people, and occasionally touching their public minds. *(This is the part of the mind that is foremost, and where first thoughts and minor memories are located.)* Though the people answer most of their questions, both Colt and Salis pick up on their nervousness.

While walking around, they take the energy readings and discover that the energy is coming from the people wearing the collars. They do several checks to be sure. On the way back, they try to ask about the collars, but no one will answer them. Everyone that they ask looks around as if frightened, and Salis picks up on the terror running through their minds. Each person quickly shakes their head and hurries off, after being asked about the collars. They people wearing the collars are even more frightened, and neither Salis or Colt can touch any part of their minds. Deciding that they're not getting any closer to finding out about them, and that they might be drawing unwanted attention to themselves, they go back to the ship.

By the time they finally do return to the ship, even with Sarah calling to remind them, they have less than an hour to get ready before Sette's driver is to arrive to get them. While Colt is getting dressed, Salis gives Sarah the information that they were able to gather and hooks up the meters for her to analyze. She then goes to her room to get changed.

At exactly eight o'clock, the hover car arrives and they meet the driver at the bottom of the ramp. This car is different from the one used earlier. It is enclosed and there is a glass partition between the front and back seats. Before getting into the car, they wait for Stephen's okay that there is no danger to them inside the vehicle.

They ignore the driver's frown at the delay, but make no move to enter the vehicle until they receive the all clear. Colt steps aside and allows Salis to enter first, and then follows her nodding to the driver that they are ready. Shaking his head the driver closes the door and takes his place in the front.

Though there was no indication of danger for them, Stephen had picked up on a listening device in the roof of the vehicle. On the drive to Sette's home they discuss the things that they had seen on their first trip into the city. They discuss the advantages of Savôn as a vacation world, and the need to see other areas. Within fifteen minutes they reach their destination and climb from the car. Adio Sette meets them at the door and shows them in.

"Welcome to my home Mr. Wood, Miss Black. This is my wife Paila. My dear, these are our guests for the evening." He says and then introduces the small silver blond woman that is entering the foyer from a sitting room to their right.

"Welcome to you." Paila Sette says in a soft melodious voice. "We are pleased to have you in our home."

"Thank you for having us Mrs. Sette." Colt smiles bowing slightly at the waist.

Paila smiles nervously at him before darting a quick glance at her husband. Seeing Adio's frown at the young man's bowing to her, Paila quickly leads them into the sitting room. "Would either of you care for something to drink? We have a lovely soft pre-dinner wine. It's gentle on the tongue and throat."

Before Colt can refuse, Salis nods her agreement. "Yes, that would be nice." She gives the other woman a gentle smile.

Returning the smile, Paila looks to Colt who also nods. Going to the drinks tray set out on a small table, she pours them each a small amount of the pale yellow wine.

Adio directs them to a velvet sofa and they take their seats. When Paila approaches with the drinks, Colt stands and takes his and Salis', then waits for her to sit before resuming his own seat. Once again Adio frowns, but says nothing about the younger man's deferential treatment of a mere woman, even though that woman is his wife.

"How was your tour of the Tower? Did you have any problems?" Adio asks after sipping his wine.

"The tour was very informative and we had no problems." Salis answers for them. She and Colt had agreed that when it came to discussing business, Salis would answer all questions. "The people we talked with were very helpful. We were very pleased by their directness and politeness."

"Good, good." Adio says and then turns to Colt. "Mr. Wood, what is your opinion of the setup at the Tower?"

Though he knows that it will anger Sette even more, Colt looks to Salis and waits for her to nod before answering. "It appears very efficient and well run."

"But . . . I detect that something does not meet with your approval."

"What Colt is not willing to mention, is the lack of female workers." Salis answers looking him directly in the face. "Throughout the whole building we saw maybe, five women. None of them holding a position of any importance."

"It is not our policy to put women in a position of importance. Women have the tendency to panic at the wrong moment." He tells her and then remembers that she is the one who will decide whether or not her people will vacation on Savôn. "I mean no offense to you Miss Black. I am sure that you deal well under certain pressures, but our women have never been able to handle crisis very well."

"I see." Salis frowns at the derogatory way he speaks about women. "Will there be a problem for our women that come here? On our world all people are equal in most aspects. We have our class distinctions of course, but those change for the better or worse for those involved. We do not keep any one group in a low position. Everyone is given the chance to advance their place in society no matter their sex." Colt places his hand on her knee and she stops speaking, realizing that she had been preaching at him. "Please forgive me for any slight or criticism I may have just made. It was not intended in that way." She assures Sette though it was meant in just that way.

"I quite understand. I assure you that should you decide that our home is to be a vacation spot for your people, we will treat all of them with the proper respect." Adio tells her with a grimacing smile. In his mind he thinks about how unlikely it was that his superiors would accept such people. They would probably infect the women of his world with this nonsense. He should never have invited them into his home. Paila would start thinking that she was better then she truly was, and then he would have to put out good money to have her reeducated and retrained. However, he had already decided he would do so before the birth of their first child.

Both Salis and Colt pick up these thoughts from Adio's public mind, and it takes all of Salis' self-control not to say anything. If it weren't for the psi's that she was sure were on the planet, she would tell them that Savôn wasn't right for their people and leave as soon as she could.

Just then an older woman stops in the doorway and announces that the meal is ready.

"Thank you Hayna." Paila smiles at the older woman with relief. "Adio, shall we go in now?"

"Yes, of course." Adio says standing.

Colt stands up next and holds out his hand to Salis. After helping her up, he steps to Paila's side and offers his hand to her as well when he notices Sette ignoring her. They had noticed when they first meet her, that Paila was heavy with child. She is now having difficulty getting up from her chair.

At first all she does is look at Colt's hand and then she looks at her husband. Adio is already headed from the room, so she takes the offered help and then quickly releases his hand and quietly thanks him.

The meal is eaten in almost total silence, broken only by comments from Salis or Colt about the different foods. When they finish they return to the sitting room for after dinner drinks. Not wanting to tire Paila, Salis finishes her drink and then stands.

"We really should be going now. It's getting late and I need to begin my report." Colt stands at her side, which forces Adio to stand as well. When Paila attempts to stand, Salis stops her. "No Paila, don't get up. I understand how difficult it is to get up when you're expecting."

Paila nods her thanks and wishes them a pleasant evening. Adio leads them to the door and tells them that his driver will return them to their ship. "Would you like me to arrange for someone to come and drive you around the city tomorrow? They can be there any time you wish."

Colt looks at Salis and then back at the other man. "No thank you. I think that we'll just walk around tomorrow. Get a feel of the city and the people. We may want someone to take us out into the countryside though. A lot of our people like camping and hiking, and we'd like to see what might be of interest in that regards."

"I'll see what I can arrange for you over the next couple of days then." Adio agrees and opens the door for them. "Good night Mr. Wood, Miss Black. Enjoy your stay."

"Good night Mr. Sette." They chorus walking out the door and down to the waiting car.

Adio returns to the sitting room with a deep frown on his face. He goes to the drinks tray and pours himself a large portion of something stronger than wine. After taking a quick swallow he turns to his wife. "You will be having no further contact with these people Paila. I do not believe that they are the type of people you should be around. Their beliefs are not such that I wish to be around."

"But they seemed so nice Adio. They were very respectful while they were here." She points out gently. "Given their age and that they were not brought up here, I was pleasantly surprised that they had such good manners."

"That may well be Paila, but they have opinions that do not fit into our peoples lifestyle and I do not wish them to be a bad influence on you. You have enough trouble accepting our way of life without outsiders putting other ideas into your head." He tells her in a condescending manner. "Why don't you go on to bed? I have a few reports to file before I can turn in."

"Of course Adio. Good night." She says more to herself since he is already walking from the room. She sighs and carefully levers herself out of her chair. Slowly she makes her way up to her room and prepares for bed.

While brushing out her hair she considers the young couple. It had shocked her that the female Salis, had spoken to her husband in such a manner and so openly. If she had spoken to him or any male in such a way she would have been picking herself up off the floor. Women in their society did not voice their opinions, especially in front of the males. Though many of her people felt this was wrong, there was no way to fight the laws that had been in place for so long. It had long been that women were considered the weaker and less intelligent of their people and therefore beneath notice. It hadn't always been this way. At one time men and women worked side by side and were equals. Some women had even been in positions of great power. That had all changed when those women refused to go to war with others for no other reason than the men wanted more land or more power. They refused to let the people be used for the greed that was over coming some of the men.

After braiding her hair, Paila carefully places a sleep cloth beneath her collar to keep it from rubbing her neck raw during the night. She had already applied the cream to heal the damage done during the day just before their guests had arrived. She just wished that there were something that she could put under it during the day as well. With another sigh she climbs into bed. She would have to talk to the others about the couple at the next meeting. They had to make a move soon or she would not be of any use to any one shortly. She knew that Adio was considering having her retrained and she couldn't and wouldn't accept that as her fate.

Once back at the ship, Colt and Salis change into lounge suits and meet in the small lounge to discuss the evening. Colt carries in a carafe of tea for them.

"Well, that was an experience." Salis says taking the cup Colt hands to her. "If there are any psi's here, it's going to take a while to get them to feel comfortable enough to talk to us. Any female psi's are going to be harder to get to talk and possibly even harder to help."

Colt moves to the seat across from her and sits. "If we do find them, we're definitely going to have problems with the government. It's control over the people is very strong and they won't want to relinquish that control, even over a few people."

"True. We would have to restructure the whole government system." Salis agrees pulling her legs up under her on the sofa. "What do you think this reeducation is that Sette was considering for Paila? I didn't get a clear picture of it from his public mind."

Colt frowns thoughtfully considering what they had learned. "It's probably something like the Federation's reprogramming. If so, it will be a painful experience. I think that we should have Sarah check their database for any information she can find. If he does decide to do it, I want to know what effects it could possibly have on her unborn child. When I took her hand I felt the child. I think that any type of shock to Paila could be harmful to the baby. It could possibly kill the child."

Biting her lip, Salis sets down her cup. "Did you pick up any psi patterns from the baby? If nothing else we can use it as a gauge on whether or not psi's are being born here."

Colt continues to frown and looks at her. "I'm not sure. At first I thought that I was picking up on something, and then all I got was mental static." He admits shrugging his shoulders and sipping at his tea. "Did you notice the slight bulge under the collar of her dress? I think she may have one of the silver collars on. It could be what was interfering with my reading."

"I noticed. I was going to ask her about it, but something held me back. Maybe we should try to talk to her without Sette around. I think we can get more information from her then from him."

"True, but we could also be putting her into danger by questioning her. We can't consciously know that, and know that we may not be around to protect her from the repercussions of her helping us." He points out solemnly. "No, we'll have to find some other way to get the information we need."

Stephen enters the lounge with a print out of the energy readings they had taken earlier. He hands a copy to each of them and waits for them to look the reports over before giving them a summary of the findings. "As you can see, there are four different types of energy readings. By themselves, they pose no threat, but after close analysis, we discovered that they can prohibit all psychic ability. We're still not sure which one causes what degree of loss, but we do know that it is possible that they could pose a very serious danger to you both should one of the collars be placed on you."

"Is there any way to counter the effects of the collars energy?" Colt asks frowning at the papers in his hands. It would be nearly impossible to get a hold of one, and then dangerous for either him or Salis to touch it and not have it shut down their abilities. He didn't want to risk it if they couldn't shut the collars off.

Stephen shifts his position so that he can look at them both. "Possibly, but we would need a collar to test before committing to an affirmative. Without a working unit, we would just be guessing. Since we have none of the four elements, we can't test even part of the combinations that might work at shutting them off." He warns them.

"Thank you Stephen. We'll try to get you a working unit as soon as possible." Salis assures him. "If that's the reason all of those people are wearing the collars, then there are enough to warrant asking them to join the alliance. With the readings Sarah first picked up, there must be close to a hundred fifty thousand psi's on this world."

"Sarah, what is the total population of Savôn?" Colt asks knowing that they needed at least five percent of the population before they can make the offer.

"There are ninety-seven thousand five hundred people on the entire plant Colt. From the calculations I have made, nearly twenty-five percent of the population may have the collars on."

Colt whistles softly and shakes his head. "All right. Then until we know otherwise, we'll act as though we are adding them to the Alliance." Colt states looking from Salis to Stephen before standing and stretching. "We better get some rest. I have a feeling we're going to need it over the next few days."

Salis stands and walks over to kiss Colt. "See you in the morning. Sarah, please keep monitoring and see if you can pick up on anything unusual that may help us. I can't believe that all those people wearing the collars are doing so willingly or that they aren't fighting it in some way to free themselves."

"All right Salis. Goodnight."

Salis nods to Stephen and goes to her room, while Colt walks out with Stephen. "Run a check on known psi energy blockers and see if there are any comparisons with those found here. If you can find something with around a one or two point difference, you should be able to find a way to neutralize this system."

"I'll look into it Colt. It may take a while. Everything will have to be cross checked at least twice."

"Do whatever you have to Stephen. I have a feeling these people need our help more then they know. Goodnight." He opens the door to his room and steps in.

"Sleep well Colt." Stephen says just before the door closes and then heads to his lab to start the cross check. He figures that it was going to take a long time before he found the right combinations.

CHAPTER 4

Over the next couple of days, Colt and Salis travel around the city checking out all of the sights as if they really were looking for a place for the people to vacation. They even travel outside the city and check the countryside. While doing this they continue to ask the people questions. Slowly they find that not all of the people agree with the laws that they are forced to live with. No one speaks out openly about it, but both Salis and Colt can tell that the people feel that the laws are unfair and cause more harm than good.

The women give as little information as possible since they fear punishment for speaking out. None wished to be reeducated, which seemed to be used more and more for each offense. Once a person was reeducated they stopped being themselves and just seemed to be a shell with a different personality.

They discover from checking peoples public minds that there are rebels that the government has been trying to capture for years. They're not sure of exactly what all the rebellion involves, but they are fairly sure that it has something to do with the people wearing the collars. It's apparent that the people hope and pray for salvation from the government that no longer really cares for its people. Many hope that Salis and Colt will bring some change into their lives with their people vacationing on the planet, but they can't really see the government allowing it to happen since Salis' people believe in letting women have a say in what happens. Something unheard of on Savôn for over a hundred years.

Taking this information back to the ship, Salis and Colt try to come up with a plan to meet with the people who wear the collars and the rebels. They would have to do it in such a way so as not to cause any trouble for any that they talk to.

The next morning, Colt and Salis are going over everything that they had learned the day before, when several men from the local civil authorities approach the ship. Wondering what could be up; they meet them at the ramp.

"How can we help you gentlemen?" Salis asks as the men come to a halt just in front of them.

Ignoring her, the man in front speaks to Colt who is standing by her side. "I am Captain Dicat of the Civil Enforcement. It was brought to my attention last evening that you have been asking the people a lot of questions."

Holding her anger in check at the man's snub, Salis answers him. "That's true sir. We were seeking information for use in deciding whether or not Savôn would make a good vacation world for our people." Colt steps back and a little away from her, ready to act should the need arise.

Captain Dicat scowls at her and tells her sharply, "I was speaking to the male woman. Hold your tongue and do not speak again!"

Straightening to her full height, Salis gives him a haughty look. "Since I am the one in charge of this mission, you will direct your questions and comments to me Captain Dicat." She informs him stiffly. "I might also suggest Captain that you change your tone of voice when speaking to me, or I shall be forced to report your behavior to District Head Adio Sette."

The Captain steps back a little in surprise at the thought of a mere woman speaking in such a manner and in a voice of such authority. He exchanges looks with his companions and then faces her once more. "If you have spoken to Head Sette," he says with some doubt, "then you know that here, women do not hold a position of authority on this world."

"Yes, we do know Captain. Mr. Sette also accepts that the final decision on whether or not we offer compensation for Savôn becoming one of our vacation worlds is entirely up to me." She stresses firmly, indicating that he was jeopardizing a profitable venture for his people. "Now, was there anything else you needed to say Captain?"

Dicat clears his throat and steps forward once again. "Yes. If you wish to ask about the collars, you must speak with the High Governor and the High Medical. They are the only ones that can tell you about them. Not even Head Sette is able to give out information on them without their permission. To do so is a violation of our strictest laws."

"I see. How would we go about speaking with these men about the collars Captain?" She asks more politely.

"You would need to have an appointment set up." Dicat informs her. "If you would like, I can set up the appointment for you myself."

"That would be acceptable. Could you set one up for later this morning? We would like to know more about them before gathering any further information."

"I will see what I can do, and contact you here." Dicat agrees.

"Very well. Your communications people have the necessary information on contacting us. We will await your call. Good day to you gentlemen." With that Salis turns and enters the ship followed closely by Colt.

Once inside with the doors closed behind them, Colt frowns over at Salis. "You took a very big chance confronting him the way you did. For all we know your speaking to him in such a way could have gotten you arrested."

"I don't think so Colt. I get the feeling that for some reason the men here fear their women deep down." She says with a very strong conviction.

He continues to frown at her. "But why would they fear them? On most planets women are the stabilizers of society. Keeping things in order for future generations. From what we've seen here, these women are so low as to not have any definition of self." He tells her as they enter the comm center and sit down.

"Don't forget what we learned about their history. At one time women held seats of power here, tried to keep the men from going to war, and did so for quite some time. The men would want to keep the women down for just that reason." Salis argues her point. "But there has to be another reason for why the women are now treated the way they are. Good or bad, we need to find out why as well as finding all the psi's."

"I don't think it's something that they will willingly tell us Salis." Colt points out reasonably and with a pointed look at her. "We may have to wait to discover the truth behind until we free the psi's."

Just then the buzzer goes off for an incoming message. Colt switches it on and listens as Captain Dicat tells them that they have an appointment with the High Governor and High Medical in less than two hours. "I will send a private car to pick you up in an hour and fifteen minutes. The driver will take you to the High Governor's office and wait for you to return you to your ship."

"Thank you Captain Dicat. We will be ready and waiting." Colt switches off and turns back to Salis. "We're all set. I think that we should wear our dress uniforms for this meeting."

"Yes, and maybe take them a bottle of mother's pink sherry." Salis agrees. "Sarah, have Stephen meet us in the lounge in half an hour."

"Very well Salis."

They leave the comm center and go to their rooms to change. In less than thirty minutes they are both in the lounge waiting for Stephen. When he enters, they proceed to tell them of the upcoming meeting, and what it is they expect to find out. Neither of the computer units like this idea, and warn them to be extremely cautious while with them.

"You should keep your comm units on at all times Salis, so that we can monitor the proceedings." Stephen informs them with concern.

"Yes, and if you should run into trouble, just say my name and I will bring you back to the ship." Sarah warns and assures them.

It is agreed that they will take the precautions and act immediately if there is any sign of danger to either of them.

They arrive at the Governor's office ten minutes before their meeting is scheduled to take place. As they wait in the reception area, they notice that the secretary is male. Looking at each other, Salis smiles stiffly.

'Even jobs normally held by women elsewhere aren't here. If there are telepaths here, we'll need to restructure the way the people think of not only them but of women as well.'

'It will have to be done slowly and carefully though. We don't want to offend anyone. Don't forget that they've lived this way for years.'

The intercom buzzes on the secretary's desk and he tells them that they can go in now. As they approach the door, it opens from the inside and they are met by a man of average height and slightly overweight with a strained smile. He also doesn't look either Colt or Salis in the face.

"Good morning. Come in, come in. I am the High Medical official Naer Briggs, and this is our High Governor Conal Toiget."

Salis and Colt step into the room and bow slightly, wishing them both a good morning. Colt introduces Salis and himself and quickly informs them that Salis is in charge of this mission and that he is her assistant.

Though the two men are slightly shocked, they react in good form to this news. The governor indicates that they should be seated. Once they are all sitting down, he asks how they have found the planet so far.

"It is very beautiful sir." Salis freely admits the truth. "The city is very well planned out. There isn't a lot of crowding that we noticed. The city is also well taken care of."

"Thank you Miss Black. It was set up for the most efficiency in all things." Conal Toiget tells her with pride.

"Are all of your cities set up in this manor?" Colt asks.

"Yes. Once it was discovered that things ran better when set up in such a way, all of our cities were arranged in the same design." Conal confirms. "Even some of the smaller towns follow a similar design, though of course on a smaller scale."

Though what they are learning is interesting, Salis decides to get right to the point of their coming for this meeting. "What are the purposes of the silver collars we've seen some of the people wearing? Though we asked, no one would tell us anything about them."

Conal frowns and looks down at his desk for several moments. "They did not answer because it is forbidden for them to do so." He informs her looking up from his desk. "For the past several generations, some of our people have been afflicted with a deformity of the mind. The collars prevent those afflicted from being a danger to themselves or others."

"What type of deformities are you speaking of Governor Toiget? How is it dangerous?" Colt asks sensing some fear of this affliction in the other man's mind.

"Dr. Briggs can better explain it. Naer, would you please do so?"

Naer nods and steeples his fingers. "As you may know, the brain consists of electrical impulses. These impulses help to control our bodies as well as our minds. In the people afflicted, these impulses are stronger and less controllable. They tend to affect others in some way." He explains carefully sure that they wouldn't understand. "The collars inhibit those impulses, while leaving normal brain functions alone. We haven't noticed any side effects to the collars nor the loss of the impulses that have been inhibited."

'He's definitely talking about psi energy Colt.'

'Yes, and they fear that energy a lot. We need to be very careful. I doubt if anyone on this planet is at a level as high as we are. We could definitely be in some serious trouble if they discover us.'

"Our religious leader told us that such an affliction was evil and should be stopped before it took over the world." Conal informs them. "Once the collar is put on, it can never be removed. The brains electrical impulses keep it in place until death."

"How do you find out who is afflicted and who isn't?" Colt wants to know so that they can avoid being detected.

Dr. Briggs pulls a small scanner from his pocket and explains how it works. "We have several groups that go out and do checks once a week and a number for the people to call if they feel that someone they know is afflicted." Planning to show them how it works, he turns it on and turns to face them. He is surprised and shocked when he picks up a strong reading. At first he looks from the scanner to them and back again unable to believe they are so strong, but he quickly warns Toiget that they have the affliction and that it is very advanced. Conal pushes a button on his intercom and requests guards and two mind collars to his office immediately. While he is doing that, Salis and Colt communicate silently between themselves.

'We need to get out of here Salis.'

'Not until we have one of those collars for Stephen and Sarah to analyze.'

'Fine. We'll get the collar and then . . . ' They are suddenly cut off as four men rush into the room, two of them carrying the silver collars. Not giving the guards time to react, Colt rushes forward and grabs one of the collars. As his hand wraps around the collar, Salis calls out Sarah's name and within seconds they are transported to the ship.

In the governor's office, all six men stand looking around. Final Toiget sits back down and reaches for his interoffice communicator. "This is Toiget. I want the alien ship detained. Put it in a tractor beam if you have to, but don't let them leave." After disconnecting, he dismisses the guards and looks at Naer. "You're sure that they're afflicted?"

"I'm sure. They're the highest I've ever seen Conal. The meter almost couldn't register their power." Naer assures him and then suggests, "I think that we should get them off the planet as soon as possible. I'm not sure that the collars could contain such power and that it would be best if we get them away from our people and away from our planet."

"But what if they should come back with more of their people? We need to think over all of the ramifications of any actions we take against them."

"Then we also need to think of what could happen if we keep them here sir. For all we know they could have a time limit for how long it should take them to come to a decision and return to their own world. If we keep them too long their people could very well come after them and we would then have more to deal with."

Both men sit quietly, wondering what they should do about this present crisis. Neither had guessed that such a problem could arise. They would have to call together the world leaders and discuss this matter. Though Toiget had final say in whatever they did, he wanted the input of his fellow leaders. For something like this they could be looking at any number of problems from off worlders as well as their own people.

CHAPTER 5

As soon as they are on the ship, Salis orders Sarah to put the shields up to full power until further notice. That done she turns to Colt and sees that he is still holding the collar in one hand and his other hand is holding that wrist; he seems to be extreme pain.

Turning to Stephen, she silently pleads for him to do something to help Colt. Stephen quickly picks up an electronic disrupter and uses it to try and release Colt from the collar. It takes him three tries before he gets it to release.

Salis takes Colt to the med unit to make sure that he was not injured in any way from contact with the collar. Meanwhile Stephen and Sarah begin their analyzes of the collar. Stephen takes it apart and they study it piece by piece in minute detail. Nothing is over looked in their analysis.

After the med unit confirms that Colt has not suffered any permanent harm, they go to the lounge to get comfortable so that they can contact Leyla and Thayer. They tell them of everything that they have learned and what has happened.

When Thayer orders them to leave Savôn and return to Calidon, they both refuse. They remind him that according to Alliance law, they are honor bound to help the psi's on the planet first.

'If we were to leave now father, Toiget could order them all eliminated out of fear that they would become as powerful as we are.'

'They could just as easily decide to eliminate you daughter.'

'I don't think so father. They won't try anything against us until they know that they can get away with it.' She assures him believing this to be true. Toiget had no idea when or how often they were to be in contact with their people. *'They have no idea about how the decision is to be made or if we need to make contact with our people at any time.'*

'How many are psi sweetheart?'

'Somewhere around twenty-five percent mother, but I'm sure that there are more than that. From what the governor and medical officer were saying, it's only been in the past hundred years or so that psi's have appeared.'

'If you stay, you stay in constant contact with Sarah and Stephen. Colt you stay at her side at all times.'

'Yes sir. We'll have Sarah contact you in case we run into any kind of trouble that they can't get us out of.'

'Just make sure that doesn't happen.'

'We will father. We'll be in touch with you as soon as we learn anything more.'

'Be safe little one.'

'Be calm father.'

Ending their communication, they both sit up. Colt asks Sarah to have Stephen bring them some energy drinks. "I thought for sure that Thayer was going to insist that we come home." Colt admits stretching his arms above his head.

"He wanted to insist, but knew that he couldn't and live with what might happen to the psi's here. He knows that they need our help. I wouldn't be surprised if he sends out a ship to help us though."

Stephen enters the lounge carrying a tray with a pitcher and two glasses. After pouring and handing them each a drink, he waits for them to finish before explaining about the collar. "With a certain disrupter signal magnified, we can use it to release all of the collars at one time. Though we would have to warn the people so that they could cope with the onslaught of thoughts they would be picking up once the collars are off."

"To do that, we'll have to go out again." Colt reminds him with a frown. "I don't see how we can warn all of the people though. There are literally thousands, and they're spread out all over the planet."

"He's right Stephen." Salis agrees frowning. "There's no way that we can warn everyone in the next few hours."

"What about warning the locals first and then having them spread the word to the others?" Sarah suggests. "They most likely have a secret comm system setup that they can use to warn the others of what's to happen."

"Are you sure that they even have such a system Sarah?" Colt asks not wanting to waste time that they may need to travel around the planet. "Even if they do, we still have to get their cooperation. For all we know they could very well accept this way of life and see us as an enemy instead of friends."

"I don't think so Colt. History is full of such oppressions and the people that try and do something to change it. Besides we already know that there's a rebel force out there somewhere." Salis reminds him of his own world's history. "There is no way that I can believe that these people accept what has been done to them. Maybe a few, but not all and certainly not those that are being forced to wear those collars. I can't see anyone willingly wearing those things."

"So how do we find the ones that want to change their lives?" Colt asks her knowing that it won't be easy. "If we approach the wrong people, we could find ourselves confronted with Toiget's men again. Not to mention placing the people we're looking for into even more danger then they are already in."

"Sarah, scan the city for any large gatherings of the people wearing the collars. You should be able to tell from the amount of energy given off if it's what we're looking for. They will most likely meet in a place not used much."

"I'll check Salis. It may take some time to locate them though. I doubt that they would gather during the day for safety reasons."

"That will be fine Sarah. We don't want to make a move until nightfall any way. As you say, any gatherings during the day would be dangerous, so they would probably use the daylight hours to let each other know of a night gathering. There's no telling how often they might meet though."

"I'll begin scanning to see how many gather during the rest of the day, and then return to scanning as soon as the sun sets and continue until just after midnight."

"Thank you Sarah." Salis turns back to Stephen. "We need you to program the med unit to alter our facial features to more Savôn standards. It may give us a better chance to move about unobserved."

"I'll get started at once. With the images that we have of some of the men who came here the other day and today, we should be able to make you both look like relatives of a couple of them." He assures them going through his memory, and trying to find the images of the ones that would best suit them both. He leaves them and goes to the med center to begin. He must find images that will blend in well with their different bone structures and skin tones. It would be easier with Salis if they had a female image to go by, but no females had come close enough to the ship for them to get a clear image.

Salis and Colt discuss how they should approach the people to offer their help in freeing them from their subjugation. They don't want to scare them into calling in the authorities and possibly putting themselves at risk.

"We should first listen and see what they have to say before approaching them." Colt advises Salis. "That way we'll know what their mind set is, and can take our cue from what we hear." He looks her in the eye and brings up what he knows will be hard for her to accept. "If we don't hear anything of discontent, we won't be able to interfere with their way of life Salis. We have to accept their decision to live as they do."

"But what if all they need is to know that it can be changed Colt?" She points out. "They may think that there is no way for it to be changed. We could assure them that there is a way. That they don't have to live like this anymore."

Colt considers this carefully. "All right. If what we hear indicates that they want that change, but don't know how to go about it, we'll step in. However, we both have to agree that it is what they want. If we don't agree, we do nothing. We can't afford to hurt these people in any way that would cause their leaders to contact the Federation and get them involved. We can't have the Federation putting restrictions on our contacting telepathic worlds. It would give them too much power to gain control of such worlds, and make our lives more difficult."

"All right Colt, but if the first group isn't clear on what they want, before we leave the planet we check another group to be absolutely sure that no one wants the change." Salis suggests knowing that others may be clearer on what they want as a group. Especially if they are well organized, which she believes they are.

"Agreed." Colt nods and then stands up and stretches. "I think that we should take a rest for a couple of hours. We may be in for a long night, and we need to be well rested and alert."

"Okay, but first I need something to eat. It feels as if I haven't eaten in a week." Salis tells him walking from the lounge.

They go to the galley and she fixes them a light meal of a salad and toasted bread with a sprinkling of cheese. After they've eaten and cleaned up their mess, they go to their cabins and lay down.

Colt asks Sarah to give them a light sleep mist and to wake them a half-hour before full darkness. "Please record all activity going on around the ship while we're asleep. I want to see what they do when we don't try to leave."

"All right Colt. I'll record all communications as well. Though their communications are pretty advanced, I can still monitor all areas without any difficulties. Even private comm lines if necessary." Sarah informs him.

"Good. Monitor the Governor's private lines, as well as Adio Sette's and the High Medical. I want to know what those three are up to."

While they are resting, Stephen programs the med unit and then works on the disrupter frequency to release the collars. He tests it out on the one they have, trying to make the time release less than five seconds. It takes him nearly an hour to get it to the point where he is satisfied.

"Sarah, how many populated areas are we looking at with collars in or around them?"

"At least six major areas and approximately twenty-four minor."

Stephen frowns trying to solve the problem of getting the signal to all areas of the planet so that they can all be released at the same time. For anyone not close enough to an area, they would have to go out and release them later. He was sure that there were those who did not live in the cities or small towns, but lived off by themselves.

"How many of the people would you estimate to be living off by themselves or in groups smaller then a town or even a hamlet?"

Sarah runs through her probabilities several times before answering. "Four or five thousand, but no more than that. I can't see the government allowing too many to be off on their own with no way to control them.

They have no population surveillance set up. From what we have already learned, they keep close tabs on the population as a whole to prevent psi's from becoming too strong. According to their history records, the political positions are inherited much the same way as the royal houses. I would guess this is to insure that an undesirable gene pool does not come in to power and change what they feel is a perfect society."

Stephen nods in agreement. The leaders of this world wanted to keep the people under control, and wouldn't want an unknown quality to come into power. He would have to discuss this with Salis and Colt later. The entire governing body would more than likely have to be replaced before they could go too far in bringing Savôn into the Alliance.

With nothing left for him to do, Stephen decides to take a short energizing period. He would build his power back up to maximum for the next several days of work that he was sure they would be doing. He wouldn't have to recharge again for another seventy-two hours. By then he would be done to about half power and should be able to take some time to boost his power again.

CHAPTER 6

When Salis and Colt get up, Sarah informs them that she monitored several gatherings throughout the afternoon and they had consisted of no more than ten people. "I was able to isolate some of the stronger energy bands and was able to track three of them to most of the gatherings. They are definitely planning something."

"Thank you Sarah." Salis says pushing her hair out of her eyes. "Stephen, is the med unit ready for the alterations?"

"Yes, and I was able to find a physical match for both of you so that there won't be much alteration needed for you to blend in with the others."

"Good, that should make it easier should we have to reveal ourselves for some reason. Let's get started. I want us ready to move as quickly as possible once Sarah locates their meeting place."

"It will take approximately forty-five minutes to do each of your alterations."

"All right. Colt, you go first and I'll have the replicator come up with some suitable clothing. Stephen, can you make us a couple of counterfeit collars with the same signature signal as the others?"

"I believe so. I'll place a small signal booster in them that will allow them to pick up the signals from the other collars without the effects. If anyone should monitor the collars, they shouldn't be able to tell the fakes from the real ones without getting up close and personal with you." he assures them.

"That will work." She nods looking back at Colt. "I'll set your clothes in your room Colt, along with a tray of food. I'll eat while you're in the med unit."

Two hours later they meet in the lounge and Stephen comes in with the counterfeit collars and explains the locking mechanism. "If you should want to take them off, your kinetic abilities will be able to unlock them. The locks are fairly simple, but not where anyone else can tell." He places the collars on them and has them practice unlocking them until they can do it in just a matter of seconds. He then takes them back to his lab to make a few minor adjustments. He would rather they were able to get the collars off within moments instead of seconds.

While Stephen is doing that Sarah tells Salis and Colt of the Savônians attempts to keep them from taking off. She explains that though the tractor beam they were using was adequate, it would not have any effect on them should they wish to leave the planet.

In the High Governor's office, Conal Toigate receives another report on the alien ship. After quickly reading through the report, he sets it aside and looks at the two men across from him. Though High Medical Briggs has been there all day, District Head Sette was only called to the Governor's office just before nightfall.

Though he's not sure what has happened, Adio's pretty sure it has something to do with Miss Black and Mr. Wood. Everyone had started acting strange shortly after their arrival, and he knows that they had come to see the High Governor and the High Medical in this office early this morning.

"They still haven't tried to leave and our scanners can't penetrate their shields. As far as we can tell, there's been no activity aboard the ship since they left it this morning." Toigate informs them, and then looks directly at Sette. "I can't believe you didn't have them scanned while you were with them that first day Adio. You have put the whole planet in danger by your stupidity."

"Sir, I take great insult in that statement." Adio exclaims strongly. "I followed the laws set for such encounters. Nowhere in the law does it state that new contacts are to be scanned for mental energy defect."

"He's right Conal." Naer puts in coming to the younger man's defense. "The law does not mention that off-worlders should be scanned at any time while on Savôn. Adio followed the laws to the letter regarding those young people. If they hadn't wanted to know of the collars we probably never would have known that they were afflicted." He points out reasonably.

"None the less . . ." Toigate begins.

"No Conal. He is not responsible for what has happened. The law is responsible for our present situation." Naer interrupts him without concern. "We were shortsighted in thinking that only our people could be afflicted with this defect."

Though he would like to argue the point, Conal Toigate knows that the doctor is right. By not making a law to cover offworlders, they had all brought this trouble upon themselves. "So, what do we do now Naer? We have to do something to rectify this situation."

"I agree, but we won't get anywhere by accusing anyone of blame at this stage."

"Sir. Why don't we insist that they go and that they agree to keep their people away from Savôn? When they're gone we place a scanner in space to check all ships before they land."

"Believe me Adio, I wish we could do just that. The only problem is that we don't know what type of response will be made in retaliation for what they surely see as an attack on them while they were in this office. For all we know they could have contacted their home world and a fleet of their ships could be headed for Savôn right now. I'm sure that they were transported back to their ship so it's a strong possibility."

They all fall silent and begin to wonder what will happen in the next few days, and whether or not their world would be able to survive. Without doubt lives would be lost because of this.

At eleven o'clock Sarah tells them that there is a large gathering in the southwest corner of the business district. There are no other life signs in the area. "The area must be closed down because I'm reading no other energy signatures in the area surrounding them."

"Can you estimate how many are gathered there?" Colt asks pulling on a dark cloak.

"Possibly a hundred, maybe more. It's hard to tell, the collars seem to be multiplying, but I can't detect how they are getting there." Sarah tells them and they can all hear the frown in her voice.

"They probably have a tunnel system that their using to keep their activities from being discovered." Salis informs her with a frown of her own realizing that such a gathering would certainly draw attention if people were seen headed in the same direction, especially ones so closely monitored. "Show us the area on the monitor please Sarah."

A map of the city appears on the screen and Sarah zooms in on the area where the people are gathering. Both Salis and Colt recognize the area as an abandoned warehouse section that Adio had told them was no longer in use because of inadequate building specifications. It was to be cleared in another month or so for new buildings.

"All right, while we're gone Sarah, you and Stephen need to create a diversion." Colt says studying the map. "We need to keep the government people concentrated on the ship until we're done. We don't need them finding us or those people. No doubt they are going to up their security for those with the collars."

"Yes. Keep track of all communications and warn us if any move is made toward that area." Salis agrees not wanting to be caught if what she thought was happening turned out to be true. "If we're lucky, we can get in, state our purpose, and get out within an hour or two. First, we need to find out what this meeting is all about."

"Do you want us to start as soon as you leave or wait a while?" Stephen questions, not wanting to act too soon.

"Wait twenty minutes and then start. Go for ten minutes and then wait another twenty." Colt tells them. "Keep doing it that way until we return unless something happens, and then do as you feel necessary without pulling us out."

With that settled Colt and Salis teleport to the warehouse and appear at the back of the building. They mentally 'look' into the building and study the layout before porting inside and making their way closer to the group. To keep from being discovered too soon, they shield their presence while listening to what is being said.

"It's not right that we're made to wear these collars." Someone to the front of the group states and murmurs of agreement are heard throughout the gathering. "There's never been any proof that what affects us has ever harmed anyone."

"There's also no proof that its helped anyone either." A male voice speaks up from the back and to the left of where Salis and Colt are standing in the shadows.

"Yeah, but how can we prove it either way when they slap one of these damn things on as soon as it's discovered that you're different in the mind?" Another male protests shaking his head at the arbitrary action.

"What about the Outcasts? They don't have collars on and there's nothing bad said about them." A woman asks from just in front of Colt.

Someone close by snorts. “They also don’t let themselves get caught. If you ask me the Outcasts don’t even exist.”

“They exist.” Salis straightens as she recognizes the woman’s voice that just spoke. “My brother is one. True, they haven’t been caught, but that’s because something inside them warns them of danger.”

“Then why didn’t it warn us?” Someone asks and the question is taken up by several others throughout the group.

“I don’t know,” Paila shakes her head, “but it doesn’t matter. We have to deal with what’s happened to us now. As long as we wear these collars some of the others see us as beneath them, and we’re not.”

“Sure, and that’s why you’re married to the District Head.” Someone scoffs at her. “Yeah.” Others chime in.

“He sure doesn’t consider you beneath him. Unless it’s in bed.” A male near Paila says with a sneer.

Paila glares at him until he looks away. “I may be his wife, but that doesn’t mean that he sees me as his equal.” She tells them looking into the faces of those closest to her. “It also doesn’t stop him from deciding to have me retrained next week.”

Salis and Colt watch and listen as several people gasp and others pale at this news. Even the man that had sneered at her pales beneath his tan complexion upon hearing this.

“If I could get this collar off I wouldn’t stay around to let that happen, and I wouldn’t allow it to happen to my child either.” She places her hands over her rounded belly.

“So what do we do? So far none of our people has figured out how to remove them without dying.” A young man in front of Paila points out.

"I don't know Creigh, but I know there's a way." She assures them.

"What about the strangers? They've been asking about the collars for the past few days." An older man asks. "They scared my Risa nearly to death when they asked her about them."

"Yeah, who are they Paila? My Gina saw them come to your house that first night about meal time." Someone else asks.

"I'm not sure. From what I understand they came to Savôn to find a vacation place for their people."

While they are discussing them Colt and Salis look at each other and talk privately.

'They definitely don't care for their situation Colt.'

'No they don't, and there are some out there that don't have collars on either.'

'I wonder where they are. We haven't picked up on any here in the city.'

'They're probably in the country or up in the mountains where it's easier to hide if someone starts looking for them.'

'So, do we offer to help them?'

'Yes we do. I just wish now that we hadn't had the alterations done to our faces.'

'We can fix them. While you were having yours done I asked Stephen if we could change back ourselves. He said it wouldn't be that hard because everything is only superficial.'

'Okay, let's do it and then approach Paila as quickly as possible.'

They start working their way slowly forward and changing their appearance. By the time they reach the center of the group they look like themselves once again.

The hoods on their cloaks keep anyone from seeing their faces until they're ready.

"We're here for more than a vacation spot Paila." Salis says stepping forward to stand in front of the other woman while removing her hood. "We're here to help you and those like you to reach your full potential."

The women in the group gasp and the men move forward to grab Salis and Colt. The man that had sneered at Paila, makes a grab for Salis, and is sent flying backwards into the men that were following him. The same happens to the two men that try to grab Colt.

"You can't touch either of us in anger gentlemen." Salis tells them quietly. "Our minds protect us from any show or thought of aggression." She looks around at the people surrounding them without fear.

"I don't understand Miss Black." Paila says in confusion. "You're wearing a collar. It stops all extra mental energy."

"That's true of a real collar Paila." Salis agrees with her and then explains. "Our collars are fakes. They were made to resemble yours so that we would fit in better here." With that she and Colt mentally unlock their collars.

"How did you find us? Did you lead the others to us?" The young man named Creigh asks, and the others begin to look around them for civil enforcement officers.

"We didn't lead anyone here." Colt assures them. "As far as your government people know, we're still on our ship at the spaceport field. We teleported here from our ship."

"How can you help us, and what do you mean to reach our full potential?" Someone asks and others around them frown in confusion.

"Where we come from, everyone is born with psi abilities." Salis informs them. When she sees them frowning in confusion she explains. "We are all born with extra mental energies. These energies are called the psi or psyche. They are a natural part of any humanoid mind and range in strength and sometimes abilities, but as I said they are a natural part of an human. A gift if you will from the Great One."

"How can you help us? The collars block these psi energies and can't be taken off unless the wearer dies."

"That's not true. They can be removed, we know how and you don't have to die to do it." Colt assures them. "We have the means to release all of the collars at the same time."

"Then do it." Someone shouts. "Yeah, do it. Get them off." Others begin to yell as well wanting rid of this government control.

"We will, but first you must all prepare yourselves. If you're not ready for what will happen when they come off it could drive you mad." Salis tells them in a loud voice. "It could also cause you to hurt or kill someone without meaning to."

A hush goes through the group at this statement and they each look at each other. None of them wish to harm anyone on purpose or otherwise. They all look to Paila, not knowing what to say or do.

"What will happen and how do we protect ourselves and others?" She asks.

Colt looks around the group as he tries to give them some idea of what they will go through. "When the collars are off, you will be able to hear the thoughts of others. Some of you may even feel their emotions. You have to be able to block out those thoughts and emotions until you can deal with them. If you don't they could basically take over your control and drive you mad."

"How long will it take to block them out and how long will we have too?" Creigh asks him frowning and wondering if it would be worth the risks of taking the collars off. He had no wish to go mad or to hurt family or friends.

"It varies from person to person. Some won't even be bothered by it at all, while others will have a much more difficult time. Once you can do it, your minds will take over and pretty much take over and do it automatically. Only those most sensitive will have to up the power of their mind shields every now and then when around others."

"Is there anything that you can do to help us through it this first time?" Paila wants to know looking around at the others.

"We can help a few, but not all of you." Salis warns them. "Our energies are high, but not high enough to help all of the people on Savôn that will be affected."

"Do you know how many there are?"

"Our computer figures that there are close to twenty-five thousand on the planet that are wearing the collars." Colt answers. "At best we could help maybe a thousand, and that's only a guess. It could be more or it could be less. We just don't know for sure."

"What do you get out of helping us? What happens to us once we're free of these collars? There's no way that our government will allow us to roam around unchecked."

"What we get is the knowledge that we've helped people that needed us. What you get is an Alliance to help make sure that this never happens again." Salis tells them standing tall and proud. "That's what our Alliance does. It helps other psi to be free and safe from oppression and slavery. It will be your choice whether or not you join the Alliance. You won't be forced to join."

For the next half hour they explain the rules and laws of the Alliance and learn more about the Outcasts and the Normals that help those collared and outcast. By the time Salis and Colt return to the ship, it is agreed that in three days' time the collars would be released and all aggressive normals would be subdued, but unharmed by anyone. Paila and the others would spread the word to the other collars and warn them while Salis and Colt contacted Paila's brother Hohl and explain what was about to happen. It is hoped that Hohl and the other Outcasts will be able to help the collared to deal with the mental onslaught that would hit them. It would take some of the pressure off of Colt and Salis to try and shield so many minds at once.

Paila had told them that the last time she heard there were close to two thousand adult outcasts throughout the world. It was possible though that there were even more than that since no one was ever able to find them to take any kind of count. If she was right and there were at least two thousand adults, then there should be enough to help the collard people to deal with anything once the collars came off.

The next morning Salis and Colt reach out to Hohl. It takes them several hours to locate him because they have to search for brain patterns similar to Paila's. They finally find him and explain what is to happen and what they would need him and the others to do.

'Can your people handle it?'

'Some of us can, but there aren't that many that can handle more than one or two at a time.'

'Have everyone do whatever they can Hohl. Even if they can only block out a little for several, it will help. Salis and I will do all that we can but we have to be careful to conserve our energy in case we're needed to counter any strong attacks.'

'I understand. I'll pass on what you've said. We will be ready the day after tomorrow at ten in the morning. Everyone will be near the towns and cities and ready to help. If you can, would you tell my sister that I love her and will be with her as soon as it's safe.'

'We'll tell her Hohl.'

Opening their eyes, they both reach for the energy drinks that Stephen had placed in front of each of them when they first started their search for Hohl. After finishing two of the drinks apiece, they stand and go to the comm center.

"Sarah, has there been anything?" Salis asks as she collapses into the chair.

"Just the normal things Salis. Though they have increased their civil enforcement patrols to every half hour."

"Have they placed any more collars?" Colt asks looking at the information Sarah is showing them on the monitor.

"No. It looks as though it's mainly a show of force. They appear to be checking all of the collars though."

"Have you been able to locate any files concerning the collars or retraining?"

"Nothing on the collars Salis, but I did find a file on their retraining. It involves both electronic and drug therapy. The whole process appears to take anywhere from a week to ten days depending on what is requested."

"Do you have any recent requests listed for the retraining since we've been here?"

"Only one. It was made yesterday morning by Adio Sette. His wife is to be treated at the beginning of next week." She informs them.

"What level of retraining did he request?" Salis asks closing her eyes and praying that it was one of the lowest.

"He has requested that she receive the highest level. It amounts to a total reprogramming. His wife will retain nothing of who she has been or what she has known to this date. She will basically be a totally new person with only the memories that they give her, and those will be whatever he decides on. He could in fact keep her from remembering her own family."

"Damn." Salis mutters surging to her feet and pacing around the room. "He plans to get rid of everything that makes her who she is as an individual."

Colt straightens up and steps in front of her to stop her pacing and takes her in his arms. "He won't get the chance atma. We'll stop him before he even gets her near the center. In fact when our little rescue takes place I doubt that she'll let him go through with the programming."

Wrapping her arms around his waist Salis lays her head on his chest and listens to his heart beating. "How can she function, how can she live with him knowing what he has planned for her? It would drive me crazy having that kind of knowledge knowing there was nothing that I could do about it."

"I know, but Paila is strong Salis. We saw that last night at the gathering. She doesn't let anything bring her down. That's why the people follow her and look to her for direction. They know that she will never give up. She may get knocked down, but she gets right back up again and keeps on going." He kisses the top of her head and then puts her a little away from him to look into her eyes. "I think that even if he were to have her retrained that her mind would fight it and regain whatever was lost."

"There's something else you should know Salis." Sarah interrupts. "While you were at the meeting, whoever was standing between you before you returned has a strong collar signal. As far as Stephen can figure out, it is one of the strongest signals we've monitored."

"That would have been Paila. We talked to her about Hohl so that we could figure out his mind set for contacting him." Colt tells her having pulled Salis back into his embrace. "Did you pick up any other strong collar signals there?"

Sarah goes over the data before replying. "Maybe twenty or thirty. It was hard to separate all of the signals with everyone so close together." She admits.

"From my calculations I would say the stronger the collar signal, the higher the alpha." Stephen informs them tapping into the monitor system to show them the graph he had developed. "It would explain why the collar you brought back clung to your hand Colt. The stronger the alpha waves the stronger the collar becomes to block those patterns."

Salis looks up and then steps away from Colt before turning to Stephen. "Could you possibly tell the alpha strengths of individuals using this and Colt's readout as a gauge? It would help us to determine whom we'll need to help and whom we can let Hohl and his group handle."

Stephen looks down at his data and considers her request. "It may take me a while to sort through them, and I won't be able to do the whole planet from our present position." He warns them with a shake of his head.

"Could we launch a satellite to give you better access?" Colt suggests thinking of the satellites they had in the hold. "We've got a Pantherian Stargazer and an Aquilian Sunspotter. Both are capable of shielding from any attacks the government might make to knock them out, and they process data almost as quickly as you and Sarah."

"It might work. I could even program them to sort the signals before relaying them back to us here." Stephen agrees, quickly running through his memory files on both satellites to be sure that it can be done. "Yes, it should work. I'll get started with the programming now." He walks to the door then stops and turns back to ask, "You do realize that you'll have to port them into space don't you? Their defense shield won't activate until they leave the atmosphere."

"We'll have to study their weight and mass, but we should be able to do it."

Stephen nods and leaves the room. Over the next few hours while Stephen is working on the programs, Salis and Colt go over both satellites learning every piece and space. By noon the satellites are in place and

Stephen is busy sorting the collar signals into alpha waves. He sorts them by the basic levels with ones being the highest and fifteen being the lowest. It is time consuming, but the information would be of great help when the time came to help the people.

While Colt is writing up their report, Salis has Sarah contact Paila. "Adio was called to the High Governor's office again. I don't know what's happening, but Adio is more aggressive than normal." Paila informs Salis after Salis assures her that no one will pick up their communication. Sarah had blocked all traces from the ship and also ones that had been placed on the Sette comm unit. Even when they were done she would continue to block those traces so as not to draw unwanted attention.

"He hasn't struck you or anything has he?" Salis asks in concern, sure that Adio Sette is a man who takes his anger out in a physical way.

"No, he wouldn't dare to. Though you may have heard the comment that because of the collar we're treated as beneath others, in some of our cases even our mates can't do whatever they like. My father is part of the High Government and though he is ashamed of my brother and me, he loves us and wouldn't let us suffer any physical harm."

After finishing their conversation, Salis sits back and frowns thinking to herself that any parent that would accept placing a collar around their children's necks for whatever reason, didn't really know the meanings of the words love and understanding very well.

The night before they are to release the collars, Salis and Colt go to the warehouse to meet with Paila and the other leaders of their group to go over the last minute details. They don't want anything to go wrong in the morning.

"We'll take care of most of the high alphas and Hohl and his people will help the others." Colt informs the group. "All of you here are highs, so we'll be helping you first. With what we've observed, you won't need our help for long and will be able to function normally within a half an hour if not sooner."

"How can you be so sure that will happen?" Creigh asks. "None of us has ever done anything like this before."

"We know that in most cases of high psi, the mind is more calm and better able to deal with new input from the other senses." Salis explains to the young man. Though he is only sixteen, his psi is at least a six, possibly even a five. They wouldn't know for sure until after the collars were off and their minds adjust to the freedom.

"Then we'll be the ones moving in against the government officials?" Someone to the back of the group asks.

"For the most part yes." Colt agrees looking around at each of them. "Both Hohl and his people with Salis and I, will try to put temporary blocks on the others so that they will be able to assist in the takeover."

"Don't forget our other friends." Paila points out to everyone. "They're ready to move as soon as they know that the collars are off. The risk to them is just as great as it is to us if not more so. If anything should go wrong, they will suffer along with us."

"We'll do what we can for them as well Paila." Salis assures her gripping the older woman's hand and giving it a gentle squeeze. "If at all possible, no one will suffer for your freedom."

The next morning at ten, Stephen sends out the signal for the collars to release. Salis and Colt immediately reach out to touch the minds of the people that they can reach and place temporary blocks up where they are needed before going to the next group.

By mid-evening the Savôn telepaths and their friends are in control of the planet. The main people responsible for the discriminations are locked up to await a trial. All would be given a fair hearing in which to plead their case. Anyone that does not admit that what they helped to do was wrong, or that still believe that what was done was the right thing, will be given the option of going through retraining or leaving the planet altogether. They would not be allowed to remain and possibly cause more trouble in the future. If retraining is desired than it would be carefully documented and the procedure done and monitored by one of the medical staff already in the Alliance to insure that no one could later say that someone was forced to have it done.

Before leaving, Salis and Colt help their new friends to setup a council consisting of both normal and psi. Every group is represented with equal say in how the planet would be run from now on. No one group would have full control over everyone ever again.

Salis and Colt take with them a signed agreement from the new council to accept the Telepathic Alliance and follow its laws and guidelines. They also have a letter of gratitude thanking them for all they had done to save the people of Savôn from the bondage that many had not realized they were in.

CHAPTER 7

With Savôn on a peaceful footing, Salis and Colt return to Calidon. They are given a celebration party for their success and praised by all for their handling of a difficult situation. It was something that no one else had run into since they started checking on new telepathic worlds.

The next day Colt and Salis are included in the decision of who will travel to Savôn to help them to prepare for the formal joining with the Alliance. Knowing the ages and occupation of each of the Savôn council members, they pick those that share common ground and outlooks.

Remembering that Adio Sette had died of a heart attack during the rebellion, and that soon Paila would be giving birth, Salis approaches her Aquilian councilor Darius Pentel.

"I know that you miss Sana and your unborn child very much Darius. Though I wouldn't presume to tell you what to do or feel, I think that you should go to

Savôn and meet with Paila." Salis suggests carefully as they walk through her private garden. Quietly she tells him of Paila and what she has gone through and what she now faces. "She's strong and brave, but she needs someone to lean on and to love her and her child the way the Great One intended. If Adio had lived, I believe that no amount of retraining would have changed him."

"How can I give her what you say she needs Salis? It would be better for her to find someone willing . . ."

"Willing to what Darius?" She asks pulling him to a stop under a lemon palm tree. "Accept a woman that will never back down from an argument, even when she knows there's danger? To put others first before themselves? When I first saw her, she reminded me of Sana. Though she had the collar on, I felt as though I could feel her essence Darius. It was like feeling Sana again. Please go with the others to Savôn. If nothing else, just go to be her councilor, advisor, and her friend. I trust you to help her, as you have helped me to learn what is needed."

"I will think on it Salis, that is all that I will promise at this time." Darius tells her quietly looking up into the sky and watching a few of his people as they fly around the palace. It was still hard for him to believe that his people had the power of flight once again after so many generations without.

"That's good enough my friend." She assures him touching his hand gently sure that she has brought him pain. "Please forgive me for causing you any pain by mentioning Sana. It wasn't my intention."

"I know this little one, and there is no pain. Only a lingering sadness that she is not here any longer." Darius assures her and gently squeezes her hand. "When will you be leaving to go to Manchon to study with your grandmother?"

Salis sighs and looks away from him. "Sooner then I wish." She admits starting the walk back to her room. "I completely forgot about it while we were working on Savôn. Since we've been back, Colt and I haven't been able to spend any real time alone together."

Darius nods his understanding. He knew that the young couple had been in several meetings since their return, giving all the information they could to back up their reports. "Why don't you ask your parents for some time to yourselves? I'm sure that they would grant you both the time you need to say a proper good-bye." He assures her as they enter her rooms.

"I've talked to mother already." She confirms flopping down on the floor cushions. "She's going to talk to father about it for me. I'd spend the whole time blushing and stammering, trying to explain our need to take our relationship to a more physical level."

"Not to mention that he will probably blow a blood vessel when he hears." Darius chuckles when she sticks out her tongue at him.

Just then they both grab their heads as they hear Thayer's mental bellow. They both grimace as they realize that Leyla has just talked to him about Salis' request. Colt teleports into the room and looks at each of them.

"The queen just told the King that you and Salis wish some time alone to say a proper good-bye." Darius explains and then grins and laughs when the younger man pales and groans before flopping down beside Salis on the cushions.

"I'm dead meat." Colt groans closing his eyes and shaking his head. "Eighteen years old and I'm going to die for love."

Salis punches him in the arm and he yelps. Darius chuckles again and heads for the door. "While you two wonder about your fate, I need to go and check on my last class of junior ambassadors. They should be done with their final essays by now, unless the King's bellow scrambled their thought processes." He gives them a wave and opens the door, then looks back at Salis. "I'll let you know my decision when you get back. One way or the other." With that he walks out closing the door quietly behind him.

"His decision about what?" Colt asks catching her hand before she can hit him again and sitting up next to look at her.

"About going to Savôn and working with Paila." She explains while kinetically getting them each a drink. "I think that they're a good match, and can help each other heal. He'll heal her wounds caused by Adio's abuse and she'll heal his caused by Sana's unexpected death and that of their child."

"You can't get your hopes up Salis. Only the Great One knows who the best matches are and when they should meet." He reminds her before taking a sip of the hot herbal tea she hands him.

"I know, that's why I asked him to think about it. I really believe that they're meant to be together Colt. Just as I believe that we're meant to be together." She tells him and reaches over to kiss him.

Colt sets down his tea and takes her in his arms. They fall back onto the cushions wrapped around each other. Colt unbuttons her blouse and reaches inside to caress her breast. Just after they remove each other's tops, they feel a tingling sensation as someone teleports them from the room.

When they appear they are in the King and Queen's private sitting room. Salis looks up from their kiss and squeals when she sees her father. Colt turns quickly around and sucks in a breath at Thayer's expression while moving in front of Salis to hind her nakedness.

Leyla grins while Thayer stands there glaring at them. While Colt stands in front of her, Salis ports their shirts onto their bodies and quickly buttons up her blouse. She had never expected her father to do something so humiliating as teleporting her from her own room without knowing if she was dressed or not.

"We didn't hear you call us." Colt explains while buttoning his shirt.

"Obviously." Thayer growls at him. When Leyla lightly touches his arm, Thayer takes a deep breath and lets it out slowly. "Leyla and I have discussed your being alone together for a week to say your good-bye." He tells them sitting down and then nodding for them to sit as well. "After what we've just seen, I fully agree that you two need to be alone without interruptions."

"We didn't expect you too . . ." Salis begins only to have her father hold his hand up to silence her.

"Always expect the unexpected no matter where you are or what you're doing." He warns them.

"Especially when children are around and can pop in at any second." Leyla says as Christa appears without warning.

Grinning at everyone, Christa kisses her parents on the cheek and then climbs into her sister's lap and pats Colt on the cheek. "Did you get into trouble again Colt?" She asks smiling at him.

It was common knowledge to all that when the King let out a mental shout or growl, it was because Colt and Salis were caught doing something that he didn't like or approve of. Usually when that happened Christa showed up and Thayer was forced to watch his words and actions. Today was no different, except for the fact that Christa was a little slow to arrive.

"No moppet, we're not in trouble again." Salis assures her sister tickling her ribs. Christa laughs and squirms around. "Father just heard something that he wasn't ready to hear that's all. You're kind of late to save us from a tongue lashing and a glare though."

"I'm sorry Lissa. Kota put me in a blocking shield. I was trying to get out when I heard Daddy growling. Then when I went to your room, you weren't there." She scolds her sister and Colt. "I felt Daddy's port and came as fast as I could."

"It's all right sweetie." Salis assures her kissing her cheek. "It wasn't that bad, really."

Thayer grumbles and the girls giggle at his expression. Leyla smiles and pats his arm knowing that both girls have him wrapped around their little fingers most of the time.

"So when do you plan to leave and when are you coming back?" Leyla asks leaning against Thayer's shoulder.

"We'll leave around five this afternoon." Colt tells her taking Salis' hand. "We should be back two or three days before the Savôn delegation plans to leave."

"Can we at least know where you're going?" Thayer wants to know. He thinks to himself, I hope that they won't leave the planet.

"No you can't know father." Salis tells him gently. "But you can rest easy. We don't plan on leaving the planet. We'll just be where no one can find us or trace us. Not even Sarah." She says with a grin.

Both Leyla and Thayer know that there are dozens of such places on the planet used as private hideaways for couples and people who wish to be alone for whatever reason. The areas block out all signals both electric and mental. The only way to reach anyone in one of these areas was to wait until they contacted you, or flying out to each area and searching for them.

"Can I go with you?" Christa asks looking up at her sister.

"Not this time sweetie. Colt and I are going to say good-bye before I leave to go to Manchon to live with Gram Royanna and Gramp Thurda." Salis explains to her quietly.

"But I want to say good-bye too." The little girl pouts laying her head on Salis' shoulder with sudden tears.

Salis closes her eyes so that her parents and Colt will know that they are having a private conversation. *'This isn't a regular good-bye Ista. It's a special one that only Colt and I can have.'*

'But can't we have a special good-bye too Lissa? You'll be gone for so long when you go to Manchon, and I don't know if Mommy and Daddy will let me come to visit you.'

'We'll have our special good-bye before I go sweetie. Just you and I will go out for a day and night. Okay?'

'You promise? Just you and me, not mommy and daddy or Kota?'

'Just the two of us I promise.'

"Okay." Christa says aloud and hugs Salis' neck tightly. "Can I help you pack a bag?"

"Sure sweetie. In fact, why don't you go to my room and start picking out some clothes for me? It's going to be real warm, so find some light clothes."

Christa smiles and kisses Salis on the cheek before jumping down from her lap and racing to the door. They all wince as the door slams behind her. *'Sorry mommy.'*

Leyla shakes her head and smiles at the door. "You must have explained it to her satisfaction." Leyla says facing her eldest daughter.

"I think so mother. When Colt and I get back, I promised her that she and I would go out for a day and night together so that we can say our own good-bye. Just the two of us."

"That sounds like a good idea." Thayer admits knowing that his youngest daughter was upset that her big sister was going to be gone for so long. "Maybe in a year we'll let her come and visit you for a month or two."

"You better check with Uncle Brock and Aunt Selina about Kota coming too." Salis warns him. "Or you may have a battle on your hands."

Thayer nods his understanding and then closes his eyes as he gets a mental message.

"Is Darius going to go with you to Manchon or is he planning to stay home?" Leyla asks while Thayer is busy.

"I don't know mother. I asked him to think about going to Savôn with the others to be advisor to Paila Sette." Salis admits.

Leyla frowns slightly at first, but then smiles as an image of Darius and a woman with a baby in her arms forms in her mind. In the image, Darius is happy and proud, and his love for this woman and child is strong and lasting. "I'm sure that Darius will make the right decision for all concerned dear."

Thayer opens his eyes and looks at his wife. "We're needed in the grievance chamber. Detra is having a problem with two of the maids and a few of the footmen that claim they should have gotten one of the recent promotions."

"It's probably the Rette cousins again." Colt warns them. "They think that just because they've been in service for so long, that they should be the first promoted. However, if you ask me, they all need to be sent home to look for different jobs. I doubt that they would have them for very long though." He snorts and shakes his head.

"What do you mean Colt?" Leyla asks him with a frown.

"Just that they're a lazy bunch who let others do their work for them and then take credit for it. Even when they do work, they do a half ass job of it and then claim that it had been done correctly earlier and that someone else made a mess of it after they were done." He explains with a shrug of his shoulders.

"What would you recommend be done about their attitude?" Thayer asks him watching him closely.

Colt frowns thoughtfully. "I'd send them to the Mesa stronghold for about six months. Moonstar and Graybear would get them into shape quickly. A few pokes with that old cattle prod of Graybear's would get them motivated."

Thayer nods and wonders if Colt had felt the touch of the prod back on Earth. Though the current wasn't very strong, it got your attention real quick. He himself had felt it more than once when he was a young man and he had first arrived on Earth. "We'll consider that as a serious possibility. From what I've heard, they've had great success with rehabilitating those with less than desirable traits since they've been here."

They all stand up to leave and Salis gives her parents each a hug and kiss. "If we don't see you again before we leave, have a good week." She tells them as they leave the sitting room.

"You too sweetheart. Have fun." Leyla says giving both Salis and Colt a kiss on the cheek. Thayer gives Salis a kiss and shakes Colt's hand.

~

Salis and Colt leave the palace a few minutes after five, porting to a cabin in a small valley east of the palace city. It is the closest private area, and the last place that anyone would look for them.

There are four cabins in the valley, each with the basic supplies that anyone would need to survive. Single storied, each cabin is built of steelwood, one of Calidon's major commodities. Each is of a different design and color to give variety to the people seeking to use them.

After opening all of the windows to air out the cabin they've chosen, Salis and Colt go for a walk into the hills before nightfall. They walk the paths in silence, watching the animals forage for food. When they reach a small meadow, Colt leads Salis over to a small stream and sits down, pulling her onto his lap.

"I'm going to miss you atma." He tells her caressing her back and kissing the top of her head. He lays his cheek where he kissed and rubs against it gently as he holds her a little tighter.

"I know. I wish that you could come with me." Salis admits quietly wrapping her arms around him. "If you didn't have to finish your training with Krander and Uncle Brockton . . ."

"There's nothing that we can do about that my love. With Brock and Krander's help, I can bring my psi tracker rating up. Maybe then your father will believe that I don't just dwell on you all the time." Colt says hugging her close.

When the sun begins to go down, Colt stands up with her still in his arms and brings out his wings. Without saying a word, he flies up over the trees and Salis tightens her hold around his neck. Though he's carried her this way before, it's still a little frightening for her. He takes them around the valley and then back to the cabin. After landing and pulling in his wings, Colt sets Salis on her feet, but doesn't let her go right away.

"I'll chop us some extra wood while you get started on dinner." He tells her kissing her forehead. "I'll be in to help in a few minutes."

Salis nods and enters the cabin while Colt goes around to the side of the building. Within moments Salis can hear the rhythmic thump of the ax biting into the wood. Quickly washing her hands, she takes out the vegetables for their salad. By the time she's done with the salad Colt comes in with an armload of wood.

Stacking the wood by the fireplace, Colt looks over his shoulder. "Do you want some meat tonight or just the vegetables?"

"A little meat will be okay. Grandmother Rachael said that my iron and protein levels are too low right now. I need to bring them up before I leave or she'll give me a couple of shots to bring them up." She tells him and then bites her bottom lip when she remembers that she had told him that she was in perfect health after their return physicals.

Colt carefully places the last piece of wood onto the stack and then stands up frowning at her. "You lied to me Salis." He says walking slowly towards her.

Salis begins to back away. "No I didn't Colt, I told you the truth. She said that I was in perfect health except for those low levels."

"Which you omitted from telling me when I asked you." He says quietly still walking towards her. "A lie by omission is still a lie Salis."

"But I did it for a good reason Colt. I didn't want you to worry about it or me." She explains still backing away from him. She bumps into the wall behind her and has nowhere else to go.

"That doesn't excuse what you did though." He tells her closing the distance between them. "I'm to be your lifemate Salis, and we share everything. The good as well as the bad. That's what will make us as one." He stops only inches from her. "What affects you will ultimately affect me as well. Loving you gives me the right to worry about you. If you want to take that right away from me . . . well . . . maybe we should get Lord Metros to perform a complete spiritual and mental purging on us so that it will no longer be an issue." He tells her continuing to look her in the eye.

Salis' mouth falls open in shock before she pales completely. Before he can move or say anything more,

Salis throws herself at him sobbing. "No Colt no! I'm sorry I didn't tell you. I didn't mean to take anything from you. Please don't ask Metros to purge us. I won't do anything like that again I promise." She clings to him sobbing strongly.

Wrapping his arms around her, Colt murmurs softly to her, trying to calm her. He hadn't meant to scare her so badly. He had only wanted her to realize that as future lifemates and possible rulers, she couldn't keep things from him no matter how much it might worry or hurt him. Once they were lifemated, such omissions could greatly affect both their lives, causing them both mental and physical harm. "Hush now Salis. I would never ask for a purge unless it was something that you wanted." He assures her putting her a little away from him to look into her eyes. "You are the other half of me atma. I would never willingly give you up."

"I love you Colt and I'll never want to give you up either." She assures him before kissing him deeply. She re-enforces her statement by linking their minds and letting him hear everything that Rachael had said to her.

"All right love, I believe you." Colt assures her again ending their kiss as his body tightens painfully. Though he would like nothing better than to take her straight to bed, he knows that neither of them has eaten since mid-morning. "Why don't you finish setting the table while I cook up a couple of mullrush steaks." He kisses her again and then waits for her nod before releasing her and going to the cooler for the meat.

Salis sighs and leans against the wall for a few seconds. Her whole body is tingling with the knowledge of Colt's arousal. She wishes that he hadn't stopped, but at the same time she was glad that he did. Though they had kissed and petted before, what was going to happen here this week was beyond anything either of them had ever experienced before.

Moving back to the table, she slowly sets out the plates and silverware, noticing as she does so that her hands are trembling slightly. Finishing with the dishes, she looks over to the fireplace where Colt is cooking the meat. She had come very close to losing him tonight, and she would never forget that any time soon. Somehow she would make up to him for what she had done.

"Do you want a glass of wine while we wait for the meat to get done?" She asks holding up the bottle of pale yellow wine they had brought with them.

"Sure, though not too much until after we've eaten something. Neither of us has eaten anything since morning, and it might affect us before we know it."

She pours the wine and carries his glass over to him. After handing him the glass, she sits down beside him in front of the fire. Sipping from her own glass, she watches the meat cook for a few seconds before looking over at him.

"I am truly sorry that I lied to you Colt. I guess that when it really comes down to it, I didn't think about what I was doing and how it would affect you." She admits with a frown. When he doesn't look at her or say anything she sips her wine again before continuing. "The only thing that I was thinking about was this week alone with you and how you might decide to put it off if you knew that my levels were low. I know now that I should have told you about it and discussed it with you."

Colt turns to look at her and nods slightly. "Yes, you should have Salis. I shouldn't have said anything about the purging though. That was wrong and way out of line. I let my hurt control me and ended up hurting and scaring you." He reaches over and gently cups her cheek. "I'm sorry that I did that to you."

Salis reaches up and covers his hand with her own. "No, I deserved it. It made me see what I had done and what I would have lost."

They smile at each other than Colt turns back to check on the meat and Salis releases his hand. Colt pulls the meat out and stands up. "It's done." He gives her his hand and pulls her to her feet. While he carries the meat to the table, she picks up his wine glass and mentally banks the fire.

After the meal they wash up the dishes and carry their wine back to the fire. While Colt adds more wood, Salis ports the cushions from her sitting room to the cabin and arranges them nearby. Though it's summer, the nights are pretty cool in the valley.

Putting the fireguard in place Colt joins Salis on the cushions and they cuddle close. For several minutes they lay there in silence sipping their wine and gazing into the fire. "Why does old Rachael always call you Firepetal?" He asks rubbing her arm gently.

"She told me once that she saw me in a dream and that I was surrounded by fire. I wasn't being burned, but a part of the fire. She saw the fire as a flower and me standing in one of its petals. Since then she's called me Firepetal."

Colt nods and turns on his side to face her. "Will you be able to change like Leyla and Thayer do?"

Salis shrugs her shoulders. "It's possible, but I don't know. In a way it scares me a little knowing that a part of me is so different. Wondering if it would make a difference to how you feel about me." She admits looking up at him.

"I can understand that." He caresses her cheek. "I felt the same when I developed my wings, but your feelings never changed, and neither will mine. The fire is just another part of you for me to love."

Leaning closer he kisses her gently at first, but as her arms go around his neck he deepens the kiss. Salis moans and pulls him closer until his chest is crushing her breasts. After several moments Colt pulls back and begins unbuttoning her blouse. Drawing the blouse from her he looks deeply into her eyes and sees the fear and excitement. Laying her back against the cushions, he reaches up to gently caress her perfect globes.

Salis gasps at the first touch and then sighs with pleasure, lifting up to create more pressure from his hands. Understanding what she wants, Colt carefully squeezes each breast. When she cries out he stops and looks up at her.

"Did I hurt you my love?" He asks anxiously.

Shaking her head Salis covers his hands with her own and presses them against her throbbing breasts. "No, you didn't hurt me atmo." She assures him huskily and reaches up to pull his mouth down to hers.

Colt kisses her deeply and then moves his mouth down her neck and kisses her collarbone. Running his tongue against the protrusion of bone, he smiles as she moans. He then works his way down to her breasts and runs his lips across her aroused nipples, flicking each with his tongue. When she cries out again and lifts her breasts up he takes the left nipple into his mouth and begins to suckle her.

Salis begins to writhe as the pressure seems to build in her nether regions. When Colt starts to lift his head she whimpers and grabs his head to place it back at her breast. When all he does is switch to the other breast, Salis sighs in pleasure and runs her fingers through his hair.

'How does that feel?'

'It feels wonderful Colt.'

'What do you feel when I do this?' He asks pulling strongly on the nipple.

'I feel as if all my nerves are connected and being pulled taut each time.'

Still suckling, he slides a hand down over her stomach to the junction between her legs. *'Do you feel it here?'* He asks pressing the heal of his hand to her mound.

At the pressure Salis raises her hips to press herself into his hand. *'Yes, there too.'*

Moving his mouth back to hers he kisses her deeply keeping his hand against her mound and rubbing rhythmically. After several minutes he feels her body begin to tremble and then she stiffens crying out as she pushes up against his hand in release.

Collapsing against the cushions, Salis closes her eyes as small shudders course through her. When she opens her eyes Colt is looking down at her. "You didn't . . ." She begins but he places a finger over her lips.

"It doesn't matter. It was enough to give you the pleasure." He tells her bending down carefully to kiss her.

When he moves away Salis notices that he's moving slowly and understands that his body has yet to feel its own release. Smiling softly she removes the rest of her clothing and mentally begins on his. When he tries to stop her she ports his clothes from his body.

Colt stands up just as his clothes disappear and he can feel the heat building in his face as his manhood springs up in relief of being confined. As he moves to cover himself he stops and gasps as Salis' hand closes over him. He closes his eyes as her fingers gently move over him. When her hand softly squeezes, he groans and moves his hips rhythmically three times before taking her hand from his body. He pulls her up into his arms and kisses her roughly before laying his head on her shoulder. Taking several deep breaths he raises his head to look at her. "We don't have to do this tonight Salis. I can wait until you're sure that you're ready. There's no rush."

Salis places her hand on his chest and slowly caresses him. "We do have to do it tonight Colt." She tells him while watching her hand on his chest. "You gave me some pleasure before, but now I want the rest. I want us to be together as we are meant to be. Giving each other pleasure with our bodies." She looks up at him shyly and takes his hand pulling him back down onto the cushions. "Make love to me atmo."

Groaning, Colt kisses her and runs his hands over her body. She matches his caresses and deepens their kiss. Rubbing his hand between her legs he checks to make sure that she's ready for him before moving over her and positioning himself between her legs. Looking into her eyes he sees her fear and desire. "I'll try not to hurt you." He assures her and she smiles shakily up at him.

"We both know that the first time will hurt me Colt." She reminds him, thinking of the pleasure instruction classes that her mother had insisted on.

Nodding he threads their fingers together and places their hands above her head. Gently he probes her opening with his tip and then quickly penetrates her. Salis cries out and closes her eyes at the burning pain and tries to pull away. Colt stiffens and holds himself as still as possible while kissing away her tears.

'Hold still love. Relax and the pain will go away, I promise.' He continues kissing her while telling her this verbally and mentally until he feels her body begin to relax under him. He waits another minute until she opens her eyes before moving slowly inside of her. At his movement Salis gasps expecting pain but only feels a slow buildup of the pleasure he had given her before.

Seeing that she is ready, Colt begins to slowly thrust into her a little harder. Releasing her hands he braces himself above her and begins to move more quickly. Salis' body picks up his rhythm and begins to move with him. Their bodies begin to gleam with passions sweat as their movements increase. Soon Salis begins to feel a tightening in her body and grabs Colt's shoulders. "NOW Colt!" She cries out as her body begins to tremble.

Feeling her contracting around him, Colt thrusts into her harder and more quickly than stiffens and cries out with his own release. He collapses to one side of her lying half on, half off of her. It is several minutes before either of them catch their breaths.

"That was . . . I don't know." Colt shakes his head unable to express himself or what they had just done. "The pleasure instruction never said anything about the loss of control."

"It was wonderful after the pain went away." Salis tells him rolling her head to the side to look at him. "Now I know what mother and Sheya meant by the little death. I thought I was dying at the end."

Colt shifts off of her and pulls her into his arms. Kissing the top of her head, he sighs and closes his eyes. "I thought so too. I'm glad that we waited until now instead of trying it when we were sixteen. Neither of us would have been able to handle this then."

"Father wouldn't have been able to handle it then either. He probably would have killed you and locked me in the tower until I was old and gray." Salis tells him laughing softly.

"I thought he was going to do that today when he ported us into their sitting room without your top on. Today was the first time I felt that he could willingly do me bodily harm." He admits with a shudder at the thought of the pain Thayer could have inflicted on him.

"I was scared there for a while too." Salis admits snuggling closer to his side.

They lay there for a while before Colt asks her if she wants to move to the bed. Salis only sighs and snuggles closer. Smiling, Colt kinetically places more wood on the fire and then gets them a blanket from the bed.

By the time they return to the palace they have decided that they can wait until Salis' twenty-first birthday to be lifemated. During the past week they had been careful to check for signs that they would have to be lifemated before then, but none had appeared. They were also careful to make sure that Salis didn't conceive. Though any child would be welcomed, they both agreed that neither of them were ready for a child.

They explain all of this to Leyla and Thayer who readily agree to everything they have decided. Leyla tells them how relieved they are by their decision to wait a few more years. "Though if you should happen to change your minds and want to be lifemated a little sooner, that will be fine too."

After seeing Rachael and passing her physical, Salis takes Christa out for the day as she had promised. They spend some time shopping and then go to a small lake for a swim and picnic. Christa tells Salis all about the things that had happened while she was gone.

"You'll have to tell me everything that happens while I'm visiting Gram Royanna."

"I will. I'll call you every day so you won't miss us so much." Christa assures her with a big smile.

"Not every day Ista. Maybe once a week will be enough." Salis warns her not wanting her to get into trouble with their Aunt Selina for excessive use of airtime. "Only if it's really something that can't wait you can call more than once. Don't forget though that we don't need to use the comm tower like the others. If you just want to talk or say good night we can mind talk. That way we won't get into any trouble for talking too much."

"But you can't mind talk that long Lissa. Not yet any ways." Christa reminds her.

"I'm sure that I can last long enough sweetie. If I can't you can tell me whatever you need to later on all right?"

"All right." Christa nods and Salis pulls her into a hug.

"I'm going to miss you little sis." She tells her kissing the top of her head.

"I'll miss you too big sis." Christa hugs her tighter wishing that she could go with her.

They arrive back at the palace in time for the evening meal and the farewell celebration for those going to Savôn. At the celebration Darius approaches Salis and her family and tells them of his decision.

"I've decided to go with the others to Savôn Princess."

"And Paila?" She asks hoping that he will keep an open mind about her friend.

"We'll see what happens and go from there." Darius promises and Salis knows that he will give the relationship a chance if that is what Paila herself wants.

"Thank you Darius. You won't be sorry, no matter what happens." Salis assures him hugging him tightly.

The party goes on for a couple of hours before it gets late and the delegates go to bed so that they can get up early in the morning for their trip. To speed their travel time they would be taking one of the new cruisers which will get them to Savôn in less than a week.

After seeing Darius and the others off, Salis and Colt go to Lord Metros ceremony chamber for the blocking ceremony that will enable Salis and Colt to be separated with a minimum amount of pain. When the ceremony is done Kasmen warns them that they will still have to make mental contact at least once every month to keep the pain from becoming too bad.

"If you can't make contact on your own, use the communications centers to initiate contact and let its energy carry yours. Don't let anyone help you to make contact, especially if your contact is three days late. The pain you feel will begin to project itself and could cause serious harm to anyone not prepared for it."

Three days later Salis and Stephen leave for Manchon in a new star cruiser that was made for Salis by her parents.

CHAPTER 8

Two and a half years later (2804)

Colt is now finished with his psi tracker training and brought his rating up to the top five. Since Salis left he has gone on three more inclusion missions of which all but one of those planets had joined the Alliance. The total number of planets in the Alliance was now up to twelve and they were sure it would continue to grow.

With only six months left before Salis is to return home, Colt decides to go to Manchon to be with her and to visit with his family. He is eager to see his oldest sister Cassandra who has just recently given birth to her second set of twins. Their family was growing by leaps and bounds it seemed with all of his older siblings mated and having children. Even his father and his new mate were having children.

"Are you ready to leave tomorrow?" Thayer asks Colt handing him a glass of juice. They had decided to have a private meal with him before he left for Manchon. He would return with Salis on her twenty-first birthday and they would be lifemated the following week. Thayer was proud of the way Colt had grown up over the past couple of years.

"Yes, everything's ready to go. I've already put all the gifts for everyone in one of the cabins. I've even got my survival gear loaded up. Da and Truloka want me to take little Carlis out and show him how to survive in the wild." Colt tells them with a shrug of his shoulders. "Though when it comes right down to it I think that its more Da's idea then Tru's."

"Isn't Carl a little young to start learning things like that?" Leyla questions them with a slight frown. "After all he's not even seven yet."

Thayer smiles over at his mate and reaches to take the hand that is fiddling with her napkin. "Age doesn't really matter love. My father started my training when I was only three. By starting when their young, their more willing to learn and more likely to retain what they've learned. It gets harder as they get older." He looks over at Colt. "Has your father thought of sending him to the stronghold up on Advacal?"

"Yes, but Tru isn't quite comfortable with the idea just yet. Da figures that if I can teach him the basics and Tru can see that he can handle it, she'll be more willing to let Carlis go to the stronghold for more training."

"I can understand her reluctance to let him go." Leyla tells them quietly, almost to herself thinking of her own children. Salis has gone to Manchon for training from her grandmother, soon Christa would be going to Kirtely for five years and only be home for visits during the summers. Saitumar was only a year old and he would be home, but . . . it was still hard to let go of another child. "She'll do the right thing when the time comes Colt. Your second mother understands that we all have to begin letting go before we're ever truly ready to."

"I just hope that I can help her to feel better about letting go." Colt admits looking at each of them.

Thayer reaches over to pat his shoulder and assure him that he would do fine. "She'll see that there's no chance for him to come to any harm, and once she knows that it's something he wants to do she'll feel better about it."

After the meal Colt returns to his room to be sure that he has everything he needs packed and then goes for a walk in the garden. Half an hour later Christa finds him sitting on a bench looking up at the stars.

"What's the matter Colt?" She asks sitting down beside him.

"Oh, nothing really little one. Just thinking about tomorrow." Colt smiles down at her as she hugs his arm. "Did you talk to Salis?"

"Yeah. She's glad you're coming. She misses you a lot. She says that she can hardly wait till you get there." She assures him.

"I can hardly wait either. Even though we mind talk every month, it's not the same as being together."

"Yeah I know. I miss Kota." She tells him sadly.

"You'll be seeing him soon though." He reminds her.

"Yeah, but only for a couple of days. He has to go back to Kirtely after the bonding with the new baby." She says with a deep sigh.

"True, but you'll be going to Kirtely soon too little one. Then you'll be together longer."

"But only for a year. He'll come home and I'll be stuck there for four more years. It's not fair Colt. Why can't I stay here? Mommy and Daddy can teach me what to know like they did Lissa."

Colt hugs her to him and kisses the top of her head. "They taught Salis because she was too old to go to Kirtely little one. It's important to them that you go there. Your mom didn't go when she was your age because she lived on Earth." He explains to her carefully. "When Saitumar is old enough he'll go to Kirtely too. You can tell him all about it when he's old enough to understand and help him to not be afraid of going away."

Christa sighs again then nods. They sit there quietly for a while longer and then Colt walks her back to her families rooms. At the door she turns and gives Colt another hug. "Thanks for talking to me Colt."

"Any time little one. I'll always be there if you need someone to talk with." He assures her returning the hug. "Good night. Sleep well."

"Night Colt." She goes in and closes the door quietly behind her.

Colt smiles and shakes his head before heading back to his own room. He wonders if when he and Salis have children they'll be able to communicate as well with them as they do with the young ones now. Sometimes it felt like adults didn't always listen to what children had to say, but he knew that it was just that they didn't know how to answer some of their questions.

Having left Calidon late in the morning, Colt sits at his ship's controls thinking about his conversation with Christa. Though both she and Kota are too young to be experiencing any of the signs of having found their lifemates, he's sure that they will one-day start showing them. He wonders if Leyla and Thayer have realized that the two children are bonded more deeply than normal.

His thoughts are interrupted when his ship is struck by a blaster bolt. Cursing his negligence, he takes evasive action. Checking his locator he sees that he is in the middle of the Entury system. He runs the ship through the computer and finds it listed as a renegade. Cursing again he opens a comm channel and tries to warn them off.

"Renegade ship, this is a Calidonian Royal cruiser. Break off your attack and let us pass. If you continue, it will be considered an act of war and you will be hunted down and destroyed."

The only answer to his threat are more blaster shots. Before he can send out another warning his shields are knocked out and he begins to lose power quickly. Just as he turns to turn on the ships backup systems the ship is boarded.

As he reaches for his weapon he is struck by a stun beam. One of his captors places a bomb on the console before they port back to their ship with him. Just before he's rendered totally unconscious, Colt touches one of their minds and finds their destination. When one of them lifts a stunner and points it at him, he quickly sends the information to Salis before the beam hits him.

On Manchon Salis is awakened from a deep sleep by images flashing through her mind and calling out Colt's name. Sitting up she reaches out to him but before she can touch his mind fully she loses all contact. She goes through the images that he had sent to her and understands what has happened to him. Getting out of bed she dresses quickly while contacting her grandmother and telling her that she needs to speak with her immediately. After receiving permission, she ports directly into her grandparents sitting room. Within moments of her arrival Royanna steps into the room.

"What's the matter dear?"

"Colt's been kidnapped grandmother. I've lost all contact with him!" She sobs shaking. "He was coming through the Entury system when a renegade ship attacked and disabled the ship. They boarded and stunned him before he could activate the secondary power system. One of them placed a bomb on his ship and then they ported him to their ship. Before they could knock him out completely he was able to get their destination and send me the information."

"We'll have to call an emergency meeting of the Alliance Council and see what can be done."

"We can't wait grandmother. It will take too long for them to gather and we need to move now." She argues.

"We can't do that Salis. It has to be a joint decision by the whole Alliance in case there is more to it than a kidnapping. There's a chance that someone else is behind this. Before we do anything we have to know who and what we're dealing with. Calidon and Manchon aren't the only ones that will be affected by this anymore." Royanna reminds her granddaughter strongly.

"Go back to your room and record everything that Colt sent to you while I start contacting the council.

We'll need as much detailed information as you can give us to go on."

"But grandmother . . ."

"Do as I say Salis! We do nothing without going to the council first." Royanna warns her and then sighs when the young girl ports from the room without another word. Thurda comes into the room and Royanna explains what has happened to Colt. Together they begin contacting the leaders of the Alliance Council.

Back in her rooms Salis flops down on the sofa and covers her face with her hands. It hurt to know that her grandmother wouldn't do anything right away to get Colt back. Stephen finds her still sitting on the sofa with her face covered several minutes later.

"Is there something wrong Salis?"

"No, nothing's wrong. Except that Colt's been kidnapped by renegades and grandmother refuses to do anything about it until it's been discussed by the Alliance Council."

"That sounds reasonable. Since whatever is done could very well affect everyone in the Alliance." Stephen nods and receives a scowl from Salis for his agreement with her grandmother. "Would it be fair to act without their knowledge and then have something go wrong and them ending up hurt or worse?" He asks forcing her to think of everyone not just Colt and herself. "Colton would not want others endangered because of him. He would expect everything to be worked out to the benefit of all concerned no matter what the cost to himself."

Salis sighs as she realizes that everything he's said is true. Colt would want them to protect the Alliance even if it meant sacrificing himself to insure that protection.

Even so she couldn't just sit still and wait for the council to decide what to do. Since Colt's visit eight months ago, they had started to feel the burning to lifemate. Though they hadn't told anyone, it had been getting stronger each time they had to make mind contact. It was one of the reasons Colt was coming to spend her last six months on Manchon. As long as they were physically close, the burning wasn't so bad.

"Stephen, would you get the mind imager for me? I have to record the information Colt sent to me for the council to go over." She asks looking up at him.

Nodding Stephen goes into his workroom to get the necessary equipment. When he returns he has Salis lay down on the sofa so that he can hook up the probes and recorder. Once she's connected to the recorder he has her close her eyes and concentrate on what they needed. Salis would have to make sure that only the information that Colt sent was recorded.

It takes several hours for everything to be recorded and changed into a visual image that is comprehensive enough for those that would be watching it. After removing the equipment, Stephen helps Salis to sit up and brings her an energy drink to help replace the electrolytes she had lost during the recording.

"I'll have Demi make copies and enhance them as needed."

"Thank you Stephen. When they're done would you have her send them to grandmother? I'm going to go back to bed." She tells him tiredly after drinking the last of the energy booster he had given her.

"When would you like me to wake you?" He asks gathering up the equipment.

"Just let me wake up on my own unless I'm needed Stephen." She says standing and walking to the bedroom. Closing the door she sits on the edge of the bed and looks at the holo-pic of Colt on the bedside table. "Why didn't you take one of the ships with one of Sarah's boxes? She would have kept you safe." She tells his image almost angrily. "Just because it's a familiar route didn't mean that it was safe to travel totally alone." Laying back on the pillows she closes her eyes and within moments is sound asleep.

When she finally wakes up, Salis has a plan to help Colt. During the noon meal she quickly stocks up her ship and has it prepared for her journey. Though Royanna has contacted the council members, she has yet to tell them of the reason for the emergency meeting. Being careful not to arouse suspicion, she finishes her preparations of furling the ship while everyone else is eating. Once that is done, she shuts Stephen down and ports him to the ship not wanting him to warn anyone until it's too late for them to try and stop her.

Whenever she is around anyone else, she keeps her plans well hidden so that no one will pick up on them. As soon as everyone has gone to bed for the night she would leave. With Demi's help she would be able to get away without the planet's detectors picking up the ship as they leave.

They leave the planet just after midnight and Demi blocks all the sensors so that it will not be known which way they had gone. She also blocks them in such a way as to not appear to have been blocked at all, which will further confuse matters as to how they had left.

Demi is a highly advanced AI unit made up of the basic parts of both Stephen and Sarah. She has a larger memory capacity and a wider range of functions and capabilities. With the information gleaned from her parent programs on different computer systems, Demi is able to enter most systems undetected. She has even been able to get into Sarah's systems a time or two even though Sarah is one of the most sophisticated computers known. Salis is very proud of her personal AI since she designed and built her with as little help from Stephen and Sarah as possible. Demi was completely autonomous from any other unit. Salis knew that she could trust Demi to follow her instructions without so many questions.

CHAPTER 9

Salis waits until they are two days out from Manchon before reactivating Stephen. When he regains full power he scowls as he looks around the ship. "Why are we on the ship and not in the palace?"

"We're on the ship and not on the planet at all because we are on our way to help Colt." Salis informs him. "I shut you down so that you wouldn't tell grandmother what I had planned. While she and the council are busy trying to figure out how best to move, we're going to gather more information."

"You are deliberately placing yourself into danger Salis. We can't allow . . ."

"I am not placing myself in danger Stephen. You and Demi are here to make sure that nothing happens to me or this ship. With you both here I have adequate protection from any danger that may manifest itself. The ship is equipped with our newest cloaking instruments and is one of the fastest in all the known galaxies." She points out then continues smugly. "I've followed father's orders to take you with me as my personal guard if I left the planet. He never mentioned anything about my needing to bring anyone else along. If he didn't think you could protect me on your own he would have."

"He did not mean in such a case as this Salis and you know that." He looks at Demi's console and frowns at her. "You know that as well Demi Dos. You should never have allowed her to leave the planet."

"I couldn't stop her Main. My programming prohibits me from interfering if given a logical request, which she gave me. All my circuits and sensors are ready."

Stephen shakes his head and goes to his shipboard lab to work on his own circuits. He knows that they were both going to need more power and stronger shields to protect Salis from what she was getting herself into.

As they travel Demi searches through the Federation's files for information on the people of Brightstar. It takes her awhile to locate the correct files, but she soon finds them and studies them carefully. According to the files, the people of Brightstar were found to be unstable and their planet offered nothing to contribute in any way to the Federation and its members. The file also states that when told that they would not be given membership the people of Brightstar began pirating star ships in retaliation. Though the reaction sounds normal, something is not computing right in Demi's logic circuits. She goes over the medical files carefully and discovers that they are incomplete. Viewing them slowly she decides that the missing information is a deliberate loss of information. The same information is not missing from every file, but everyone is missing something different and she can separate them into groups by what they are missing. She also discovers that when certain entries are combined they indicate that the people have an unusual molecular structure. Though she's run several simulations, she has yet to figure out what that structure could be. Before telling Salis about it she goes over everything again to make sure that she hasn't missed anything.

When Salis gets up in the morning, Demi goes over what she had found and the conclusions she has come up with from that information. "That a people who have never shown any aggression in the past would do so now is not logical. I checked other Federation planet computer systems and found several references to a traveling band of actors that come from Brightstar. There was never any indication that they caused any problems."

"Could the Federation have branded them renegades because they refused an offer?" Salis questions her remembering her father mentioning that the Federation did not like to be turned down if there was something that they really wanted.

"It's possible, but I' couldn't say for sure without knowing what was offered and refused." Demi informs her. "It could also be a cover-up for something the Federation is doing and don't want anyone else to know about. They could be being used by the Federation's orders and have no choice in the matter."

"But surely they would have sought help from an outside force? Everyone knows that the Federation doesn't run everything. Our Alliance is proof of that."

"They may have some kind of hold over the people to keep them from seeking help." Stephen points out having listened quietly until now. "If they were a peaceful people, just a threat to do something could be enough to keep them in line."

"What about the medical reports Demi? Was there anything in them that could help us to figure all of this out?"

"I've found that their molecular structure is unusual by Federation standards. I haven't been able to figure out what makes them so unusual from the simulations that I've run. The cell structure is definitely different from anything we have on file." She puts several files on the monitor for Salis and Stephen to look over. "There are several entries missing in the files also and they were deliberately omitted." She lights up each of the missing entries. "Without the information from those entries there is no way to know what physical mass and composition we are dealing with."

Salis and Stephen carefully go over the information and see what Demi means. There is no indication of cell type or density. There is also no information on the chemical composition of the cells. From viewing other records they all agree that the missing entries was a deliberate act of omission.

"All right Demi, please keep trying with the simulations. Try adding the missing elements with known parameters and then increase and decrease them as you deem necessary. With luck you may find the missing pieces needed to discover what we'll be up against." Salis yawns and stands up stretching. "I'm going to get some more sleep. Wake me if either of you come up with anything." She goes to her cabin and takes a shower before collapsing onto the bed. Before she can go to sleep she hears Christa, who is now seven, calling to her.

'Lissa I know you hear me.'

'What is it little one?'

'Mother and Father are not happy with you. Neither is Grandma Anna. They're all disappointed that you left the way you did.'

'I know little one, but I had no choice. It would have taken the council too long to meet and even longer to make a decision on what to do. Colt needs help now, not in the next month or so.'

'You don't believe it would have taken them that long Lissa. They didn't even plan on meeting physically to talk about what to do. They know how serious everything is.'

'Knowing and acting upon that knowledge are two totally different things Christa. By my going out right away, I may give the council more time to come up with something that will insure that this never happens again.'

'You know that they can't do that Lissa. Nobody can tell pirates what to do.'

'That's just it sweetheart, I don't believe that they are really pirates or rebels. Colt's ship was destroyed instead of taking it to use for their own purposes later. No I think whoever these people are that took Colt are working for the Federation. We need to let them know that the Telepathic Alliance won't stand for such actions any longer and that we will do whatever necessary to see that it doesn't happen again.'

'Just don't be afraid of what you'll have to do to make that happen Lissa. Soon you have to release your inner fire and finish your transition.'

Salis frowns hearing her little sister discussing something that she herself as yet didn't understand. *'What do you mean Christa? How will I release my inner fire?'*

'Trust in it and in yourself Lissa. Never doubt yourself or those you truly love. When it's time you'll know what to do and how to do it.'

Feeling Christa yawn, Salis assures her that she'll remember, then tells her to go to sleep. After ending their conversation she lays back and wonders even more at Christa's knowledge and understanding. Even though she is only seven, at times her mind is like an adult's in her thinking and language. If not for her size and childish ways, Salis would wonder who the eldest sibling was.

No matter that Christa was younger, Salis had learned that her little sister was wise beyond her years and had a knowledge way beyond that of any adult in their lives. Something that she only let out on rare occasions, and then usually only to those who needed the knowledge that she had and would accept it coming from a child. Salis herself may question some of the things her baby sister told her, but she would always trust what she had to tell her. She was given the knowledge to share and to teach and Salis knew that she had a lot to learn and that it didn't matter where she learned it as long as she did learn it.

Though she fears her inner fire, she knows that it will always be a part of her and that it must be released if she is ever to be all that the Great One has meant for her to be. He hadn't given her that special gift for no reason. Salis just had to figure out what that reason was and then to fulfill it to the best of her own ability.

They are nearly to Brightstar when Stephen notices a shadow image on the rear scanners that Demi hadn't mentioned and decides that she had not been checking those scanners. Though it could be just what it appears, Stephen decides not to take any chances.

"Demi Dos. Use your personal scanners to check the image behind us."

Demi checks the image and at first it appears to be a particle shadow of their own ship. Upon closer inspection she discovers that it is not their shadow but another ship. Checking the scanners logs she sees that it has been behind them for almost three days. Realizing that she should have caught it the first day, she programs herself to check all possibilities at all times no matter how unimportant it may seem at the time. She enlarges the image and cleans it up so that they can see it more clearly. That done, she puts the image on the monitor in front of Salis and Stephen.

Salis studies the image and then cries out when she recognizes it. She looks more closely to be sure and places a hand over her mouth. Looking up at Stephen she nods. "It's the same type of ship that attacked Colt." She looks back at the monitor and frowns wondering why they haven't attacked. "How long did you say that it's been following us Demi?" It made no sense for them not to have done something before now since Demi had not taken any evasive movements.

"About three days Salis. I apologize for not noticing it immediately it took up position behind us. I did not calculate that they would come up on us from behind.

I figured any confrontation would come from the front or either side."

"I don't blame you Demi. It never occurred to me that they would do something like this either. I wonder why they did."

"They may have done so to keep us from turning back." Stephen points out to them. "Even so, none of this makes any logical sense. Why would they take Colton? There is nothing the Federation could know of his position or his relationship with you or any of the other royal families of the Alliance. He has never been present at any of the functions involving the Federation except as a guard."

Salis frowns again as she realizes that he's right. Then she remembers Denral. "He hasn't, but his father has. That's what would make him a target. Denral is a High Lord of Manchon now and has been taking the Alliances answers and grievances to the Federation as our spokesperson. They may have decided that they want Denral under their control. What better way to do that then to take one of his children?"

"They wouldn't know what strength Colton had as a psi though. None of the people in the Alliance have their psi strengths recorded in anything that the Federation might see. Any time that the Alliance has helped them, those assisting where listed as two or three psi levels lower then they truly are to give them an added advantage should it become necessary. He could very easily get away given the chance."

"But he hasn't Main." Demi points out. "If he had gotten away he would have contacted Salis by now."

"Demi's right Stephen, and if he were dead the burning would have stopped, but I still feel it deep within me." Salis tells him. "They must be blocking him somehow."

"They would have had to have done so before he regained consciousness, otherwise he would have sent more information." Demi agrees.

"Demi, probe that ship and find out what type of weapons system they have and how their ship is powered." Salis tells her standing and pacing around the cabin. "I want to know everything there is to know about that ship before they make contact. Do it without their knowledge."

"I'll do my best Salis."

"Why don't you go eat something Salis. It may take her a while to get into their systems." Stephen suggests sitting in the chair. "I'll go over the information as she gets it and see what we can do to disable them before they can do us any harm."

Salis nods and goes to the galley and fixes herself a salad. Sitting at the table she tries to remember if at any time in the Federations presence she and Colt had shown any affection towards one another. As far as she could remember they hadn't. All contact between them at those times was strictly as a princess and a guard. She realizes that he could have been taken because of the ship he was flying at the time. Though it was his ship, it was listed as a personal royal cruiser. Whoever took him might have thought that he was part of the royal family or a member of the council. They were usually the only ones to use those cruisers.

After finishing her salad, Salis goes to take a shower and change. When she's dressed she lays down on her bed and tries once again to reach out to Colt. Though she doesn't make full contact, she does feel a tingling that lets her know that his brain is in an active state. Though she had told Demi and Stephen that she knew Colt was still alive, she was glad to have it confirmed.

Meanwhile Stephen goes over the information Demi has gathered on the other ship. The weapons are common disrupters and lasers that Salis can disable easily. The only problem he can see will be to shut down the computer system and engines, while keeping the ships life support systems going.

"Demi, can you get their computer to shut down all functions except for life support?"

"Yes I can, but I'll have to take out their backup system first. Can Salis handle the weapons? I can't touch that system without setting off their alarms."

Stephen frowns about the alarm system on the weapons. It was unusual for a ship of that size to have such a system. "She can handle the weapons and not bother any of the alarms. We will have to see what she wishes to do with this information." He turns on the ships internal comm unit. "Salis, we have all the information."

"Thank you Stephen. I'll be there in a couple of seconds." Salis sits up and then stands. After straightening her clothes she ports to the bridge. "What do you have?"

Stephen urges her to sit before explaining. "The weapons are basic. You've disarmed their kind before. The computer is more complex and controls all other functions. Demi can shut down the system and still leave on the life support. What do you want to do now?"

Salis looks at the monitor and studies the other ship. "How far behind us are they Demi?"

"Approximately two point seven hours."

"All right, stop the ship and we'll wait for them to came into closer range. When they're close enough we'll shut down their systems and bring them aboard for questioning. Stephen, I want you to have a stunner ready just in case they're able to get through the shield I put up. I'll keep it up until I'm sure that we'll be safe without it. We won't take any chances. The minute you think that something is going wrong fire upon them. We'll deal with any misunderstandings after they're secure."

"We're at a full stop now Salis. The shields are at maximum power and the other ship has increased speed. They will now reach us in approximately thirty minutes at their present speed."

"Thank you Demi. Let us know as soon as they are within range or if they should arm their weapons. I want their ship as close as possible before we disable it just in case something should go wrong. I'll put the shield in place before we transport them over."

The wait for the other ship seems endless, but soon Demi tells them that they are close enough should anything go wrong. Salis disables the ship as soon as it's in range and puts up her shield. Once the shied is in place she has Demi transport the four man crew from the other ship. When the crew appears with stunners in hand, Salis strengthens the shield around them.

For several minutes both groups just stand there staring at each other. Demi closely studies their physical forms and does a quick medical scan of each of them. As she is scanning, she picks up minute changes in their molecular structures and then in their physical appearance and mentions it to Salis.

"I'm not sure what is happening, but their cells are undergoing some type of change. I'm also picking up a change in their physical appearance."

"There's nothing here that could be affecting them is there?" Salis asks speaking softly.

"No, there's nothing. The only difference that there is that I know of is that our cabin temperature is two degrees warmer than theirs. Not anything that should bring about these type of changes."

Salis watches them more closely and notices the physical changes taking place in each of them. One changes into a leopard with all the markings, another transforms into a black wolf, and the other two turn into birds of prey. Within minutes their physical appearances are totally changed from their human forms. Not showing any fear to what she has just witnessed, Salis assures them that they are in no danger from her or her companion.

"We're only here to find a friend that was taken by your people. We don't want any trouble with your people. We just want him returned to us. Our people are peaceful and wish only to live in harmony with those around us."

The four look at each other and then return to their human forms. The oldest of the four steps forward, but stops when Stephen steps closer to Salis and a little in front of her. "We too mean no harm to you."

Salis moves to stand at Stephen's side. "Why were you following us?"

"Only to be sure that you were not coming to attack our planet." He assures her holding up his hands in an open gesture.

"And what about my . . . our friend, why did your people attack him and destroy his ship? He wasn't even headed toward your planet like we were."

"We did not intend to destroy his ship, only to disable it. He was taken only to get your people's attention, nothing more."

Though she knows that he is not telling her everything, Salis senses no real malice in any of them. Trusting them not to do anything to threaten her, she lowers the shield from around them while raising her personal one and strengthening it. "Please have a seat. Stephen, would you please get us all something to drink?" She waits for the others to sit before taking her own seat.

"We are Emorpha and we need your help. Our people are peaceful as well, but we are called rebels and renegades because our beliefs are not the same as the Federations." The eldest explains to her as the one called Stephen hands them each a fruit drink. "We would like to ask your help in getting the label of renegade removed. It was decided that the only way to get your Alliances attention was to take one of your people. Our leaders felt that because of our standing as renegades that your leaders would not willingly listen."

"That may well be, but trying to get our attention by taking one of our citizens was not the way to go about it. Unless your people can assure us that our citizen is safe and unharmed, the Alliance will take action against your people." She warns them though she knows that this was the last thing that any of them wanted.

"Your citizen is safe and unharmed my lady. If you will but listen to our leaders, I am sure that you will see how much we are in need of your help."

Salis considers him carefully before speaking quietly to Stephen in their special binary language. “What do you think about what he’s told us so far?”

“He has not told us everything. What he has said so far is true, but I believe that the Federation is more involved than just labeling them as renegades.”

“Do we talk with their leaders and see what they have to say about all of this, or do we just go in and take Colt and leave them to deal with their own problems?”

“We get Colt and then listen to their leaders. If they have nothing to hide they well agree to return him to us. I would also like to hear what he has to say. I believe that he will have some information by now that will help us to better understand the situation.”

Nodding at his advice, Salis looks at the Emorpha. “All right. I will talk to your leaders and hear what they have to say, but I want our friend present when we arrive. I want to see for myself that he is in good health and has been treated well. That he wasn’t seriously injured when he was taken.”

The Emorpha look at each other before nodding to each other in agreement. “Thank you my lady. We will guide you the rest of the way to our home and guaranty your safety. I will also guaranty that your friend is there to greet you so that you will see that he is safe and unharmed.”

“Very well. We’ll send you back to your ship and follow you the rest of the way. Be aware that we will be monitoring all communications between you and anyone else.” Salis warns them and lifts her hand to forestall Stephen’s objections to her giving them such a warning.

"We understand my lady." The elder answers and the four of them stand as one.

"Full function and control of your ship will be returned to you as soon as you are back on board. Your weapons however will remain off-line until we reach your world or we should encounter trouble." Salis tells them standing and indicating that they should return to the area that they had appeared in. Once they are in position Demi transports them back to their ship and returns control to them.

"You should not have mentioned that we would be monitoring their communications Salis. They could have said something that would have given us something more to go on."

Salis turns to look at him. "I don't think so Stephen. If I were them, I would expect to be monitored. Besides, until we know for sure that the Federation is behind all this, I want to deal as honestly as possible with them as possible without endangering us, them, or Colt."

"They could always use a sub channel or encoded message to create a warning." He points out.

Demi interrupts. "I am monitoring all of their communications systems on all levels Main. I even have their inner ship comms monitored to be sure that they aren't planning anything for before or after we land. With me monitoring their inner comm system I can hear everything that is said without them even having to use that system. Not only that, but while they were here I studied their vocalizations and word inflections along with their pulse rate and respiration's. Should they attempt to secretly send a message while communicating on any of their units, I'll be able to pick up on it and shut them down within moments."

"Good. Record everything you hear from now on. I have a feeling we're going to need it later." Salis tells her straightening her outfit. "I need to contact Christa and have her relay a message to mother and father. Let me know immediately if they try anything." She goes to her cabin and lays down closing her eyes. Slowly she relaxes her mind and body.

'Christa, I need you to relay information to mother and father.'

'What is it Lissa? They've been really worried about you.'

'Tell them that the people who took Colt call themselves Emorphas. They have the ability to change their physical form. From what they said the Federation labeled them renegades because their beliefs don't coincide with those of the Federation.'

'Do you believe them?'

'A little, but not completely. There's a lot that they didn't say that leads me to believe that in some way they may be working with the Federation. They say that they want the Alliance's help in clearing themselves as renegades. I believe that on some level they truly do want our help with the Federation, but I can't seem to figure out how or why.'

Christa remains quiet for several moments. *'Do you want me to tell father to come now? He already has the ships ready to leave as soon as you need them.'*

Salis thinks about it for a second. Knowing her father he was ready to leave now whether she wanted him to or not. *'Tell him to come, but not too quickly. I want to be absolutely sure that what we're dealing with calls for the type of force I'm sure father convinced the council is needed. With them on the way, I should be able to contact father to let him know when to move in or to wait.'*

'All right. Is there anything else that I should tell them?'

'Tell them that I'm sorry that I did it this way, but I had no choice. I'll accept any punishment they and the council think I deserve.'

'Okay Lissa, be careful. May the Great One gently guide you through your decisions and actions. Open yourself to Him and He will help you whenever you are in need.'

'I will Ista. Take care little sis.'

Opening her eyes Salis looks up at the ceiling and then asks Demi for a report. Demi tells her that the Emorpha had contacted their people, but hadn't tried to send any secret messages. Thanking her Salis closes her eyes and falls into a deep restorative sleep. With all that she has had to do over the past couple of hours she would need a large restorative when she got up again.

"I think that we should just go in and deal with this straight out. We can't allow anyone to think that they can control us by threatening even one of our people without some kind of retaliation. If we do, we will just be asking for it to happen over and over again." Thayer growls slamming his fist down hard on his desk causing things to rattle after Christa tells him what Salis had told her.

"Lissa's not saying to do nothing Daddy. She just wants you to wait until she has all the information." Christa tells him quietly while gently placing her small hand on his shoulder when he sits down at the desk. At her touch Thayer's anger begins to fade and he sighs deeply. When she knows her father is once again in control of his anger Christa continues. "In their minds they had no other way to get our attention. Maybe someone told them that no one would listen to them, that we wouldn't listen. Lissa just wants to be sure that we don't retaliate in blindness. What they did was wrong, but to punish them without knowing everything would be just as wrong Daddy."

Leyla looks from her mate to her young daughter. Though Christa was only seven, she showed the wisdom and maturity of someone much older. "She's right Thayer. If we go in shooting without first having all the information we can get, then we'll be no better than some of the people that run the Federation. Go, but wait for Salis' call before you do anything. Have faith in her judgment, know that she would never endanger the lives of our people or other innocents just to save herself from the pain of losing Colt."

Thayer closes his eyes and breathes deeply several times before nodding his agreement. "We'll go out and wait Leyla, but I just hope that no one suffers unduly for it. Not even our daughter." Though he was angry with his oldest for what she did, Thayer could understand her concern for her chosen mate. It didn't excuse what she had done, but it was something that any of their people would have done if put in the same situation.

CHAPTER 10

They are almost to Brightstar when Christa contacts Salis and tells her that their parents want her to listen carefully to what is both being said and not being said, and to make sure that she questions the Emorpha's thoroughly on everything.

'Mother will have someone check out whatever you find immediately. Whichever way it goes she plans to have them checked out thoroughly through the Alliance contacts.'

'All right, I'll do what I can and have Demi begin sending the information as soon as we can get it.'

Meanwhile Demi activates her android body and does a systems check to make sure that everything is in good working order. Both she and Stephen will go out with Salis to record and analyze everything that is seen and heard. They will also be better able to protect her with both of them present. Once she's certain that her body is in top form, Demi transfers her necessary functions to it. Carefully she moves her limbs to gain control before attempting to stand. Once on her feet she does several coordination moves.

Demi's ship-self lands and scans the area for Colt. It takes several minutes before she can locate him and she notices that his biorhythms are not normal. She double checks them before mentioning her findings to Salis.

"Though he's standing and his eyes are open, his rhythms are those of someone in a semi-comatose state." She warns her.

"Could they have him drugged?"

"I can't detect any chemicals in his system."

Salis reaches out to touch his mind and is only slightly reassured when she finally touches it. She tries several times to talk with him, but gets no response. She's not even sure if he can hear her. There is no sign that he is even feeling her touch.

"I can't reach his mind Demi. Would you check for any electronic blocks?"

"Scanning now Salis." For several moments all is quiet. "I can detect some type of electrical interference on a low alpha level. The only way it could be affecting Colt would be for it to be on his body." Deciding there is nothing they can do until they see Colt, they decide to wait a little longer.

When they finally leave the ship, Stephen leads the way out followed by Salis and then Demi. As soon as they are all out Stephen and Demi put up a shield to protect Salis so that she doesn't have to use up any energy generating her own shield. The frequency of the shield is such that neither the Emorphas or the Federation would be able to detect it unless they should happen to fire upon them or get too close.

As they approach the area where Colt is standing with several Emorphas, Salis notices his totally blank expression. Though she knows he's seen her, his expression never changes. Using her bio-link with Demi's physical form, she tells her what she's noticed. "I noticed it too. There was a slight fluctuation in his biorhythm when he first saw you. I believe that he's controlling his biorhythm for some reason. We need to get him back to the ship as soon as we can."

When they reach the midpoint Stephen stops and steps slightly to the side so that Salis and Colt can clearly see each other. He scans the area to note the position of the Emorphas. The three of them watch as one of the Emorphas leans closer to Colt and speaks softly into his ear. Colt turns his head slightly to look at the man beside him before nodding and facing forward again. The man says a few more things and a few moments later Colt begins to stiffly walk forward.

As Colt walks slowly towards her, Salis carefully looks him over. His clothes are rumpled but clean, his dark brown hair has grown out more since the last time she saw him, and it now reaches just past his shoulder-blades. What gets to her though is his light brown eyes, they are slightly dull and his copper skin tone looks almost gray. When she looks at his hands she notices a band around his wrist and frowns. It was not something that he would willingly wear, so she knows that it must be what is blocking him from her.

Colt walks away from his captors and walks slowly towards Stephen. Being careful so as not to draw any unwanted attention to what he's doing, he points to the band on his left wrist and then grabs his arm just above it. It was a signal that they had worked out a few years ago to indicate that something on his body was a danger to Salis.

Though Stephen picks up on the signal, he isn't quick enough to realize that it is a danger to Salis. They hadn't had to use the signal since they came up with it and so his processors where slow in making the connection. When he finally hits on the signal it's too late and Colt is close enough to temporarily deactivate both him and Demi.

When he's in range Colt says the command that will deactivate both androids for two minutes. It will give him enough time to get Salis and pull her away from them before they reactivate. He wished that he could tell her what was happening but there wasn't much time. Though the Federation's man had a slight hold on him, it wasn't one that he couldn't break. Something was going on here with these people and he needed to know what. He was sure that if left on their own they would never have done this. For the few moments that he had before the band was put on him, he had gotten the impression that their minds were foggy and confused. They could see themselves doing things, but couldn't understand why they were doing them.

He needed time to get Salis to understand that it wasn't the people of this world that were their enemies, but yet again the Federation. Colt needed her to see for herself what they were going through. They have to come up with a plan to stop the Federation and save these people from whatever plans they had for them. Pulling her close and away from Demi and Stephen, he quickly whispers in her ear. "Trust me."

Salis looks up at him and can see the pleading in his eyes. With barely a nod she lets him know that she does.

Quickly, before the others get too close he tells her. "Tell Stephen and Demi to return to the ship that we will call them when we need them. It's the only way to keep them safe."

When Stephen and Demi reactivate Stephen uses him connection to speak to her privately. "Demi you must analyze that band on Colt's wrist as quickly as possible."

Demi works quickly and carefully examining everything until she has all the information she'll need. Before she can do anything with it, Salis talks to them in binary.

Before the Emorphas get too close, Salis looks back at Demi and Stephen and speaks to them in binary code when she sees that they have already reactivated. "Go back to the ship. Do nothing until we contact you." She looks directly at Stephen. "*Do not,* contact my father."

Just as the Emorphas surround them, the androids turn and return to the ship. Though they both fight it, they can't override her binary command. They secure the ship and record everything that is happening outside. "Why did she do that Main? It makes no logical sense. Moreover, why did Colt deactivate us? We could have gotten him back and safely onto the ship."

Stephen studies what is happening outside the ship as he answers her. "Colt must have needed more time under their control and needed Salis' help. The band on his arm is some type of restraint, but not strong enough to really control him. I believe they will be gathering more information for us to work with. The reason for Salis' actions were to protect us and the ship if something should go wrong."

"But why tell you not to contact her father?"

"That's just it Demi. All she said was not to contact her father, she didn't say not to contact the King." He points out. He watches as the Federation's man steps out of the shadows of one of the buildings. "We're to give them five hours, and then contact Thayer if they haven't returned to the ship. What did you find out about the band he was wearing?"

Demi looks at him and then returns her focus back to the monitor. She would track Salis' every move. Luckily they had a special bond that allowed Demi to always know where she was no matter the distance or any type of electronic blocker. She just hoped that Salis would remember to turn on her personal recorder so that Demi could hear and see what was going on around her. "It's one of the Federation's newest psi blockers. I picked up their signature codes right away. Every band is designed to inhibit both psi and conscious thought."

Zooming in on the image, Demi and Stephen watch as Salis and Colt are lead to were the Federation's man is waiting. He says something to them and then nods for the Emorphas to take them to one of the other buildings. Watching them walk away he turns and looks at the ship. Demi is sure that he is trying to figure out a way to get on board so that he could go over her computer files to find out whatever he can about the Alliance. She wonders if they could use that against him, but says nothing to her father until she can figure out everything that could go wrong with letting him into the ship unrestrained.

Colt and Salis are taken to the same building Colt has been kept in since his capture. Once the Emorphas leave after placing a band on Salis, she turns to him and signs wanting to know if there are any listening devices or cameras.

"None that I've been able to sense." Colt tells her softly. "I'm sorry that I couldn't give you some kind of warning atma. I just couldn't take the chance of Stephen or Demi reacting to a perceived threat to you and harming one of these people. I don't think that they have much choice in what's happening."

Salis nods having already come to that conclusion herself. "What about the Federation's man? Have you found out anything about him?"

"He's a psi four. He's been here for a while and has some control over the people, but it's not complete. Every now and then I can feel them fighting it." He tells her taking her hand and drawing her closer. He looks into her eyes. "I wish that you hadn't heard me. That you never knew what was happening."

Salis reaches up and cups his cheek. "I think that I would have known any way atmo. We're too close for me not to." She smiles softly up at him. "And if I hadn't and found out later after you escaped I would have kicked your butt for not letting me know what was happening."

He chuckles and pulls her to him in a tight hug. "I'd let you do it to just so you would feel better and know that I was alive."

Slapping at his shoulder she lays her head on his chest. "What does that band do? Why couldn't you hear me out by the ship?"

"It's an inhibitor, but it also reads psi levels. I've had to keep my biorhythms low so that they can't get a true reading and it can't adjust to completely cut me off." He kisses the top of her head and then leans back to look her in the face. "I probably could have gotten it off myself but then they would have known my psi strength, which would have given them a base to figure out what strengths your family has. They would know that no leader would have someone stronger then themselves that close to their family unless they were stronger still."

Salis looks at him and realizes that he's right. All they needed was someone that was always with the family to figure out what the psi strength of the leaders would be. "Demi, I know you can hear us and I know that you've studied the bands. Neutralize them so Colt and I can get out of here."

Using her connection with Salis, Demi quickly neutralizes the bands and confirms it in Salis' mind. "Are you coming straight back to the ship?"

"Not right away. We're going to look around first. We've got the bands off so reactivate them and set them as if we still have them on. It will buy us a little more time to look around and see what we can find." She turns back to Colt. "Do they have any kind of schedule as to how often the check on you?"

"They shouldn't be back for a couple of hours. Their watcher is probably contacting his ship right now to let them know that he has you too. He has a Federation high frequency communicator that he's been using every three days. I'm not sure how close it is to the planet."

"Should I have Demi block him?"

"No, let him contact them for now. I think he'll put them off for a while so that he can interrogate you first. He's seems the type to want as much power as he can get and he won't want to hand either of us over until he has as much information as will benefit him with his superiors. Have her block anything else after his initial report."

That done, they leave the building and cloak themselves to wander around the village unnoticed. After a couple of hours they return to the ship just as the Emorphas are headed to the building where they had been placed. They watch as two people enter and then rush out when they find them gone. Looking around, one of them heads to the building where the Federation's man had entered, the other continues to look around and then looks over at the ship.

Dropping their cloaks Salis and Colt nod to the man and then watch the other come out with the psi four. The first man points in their direction and they smile at the shock on the psi's face that they had escaped without him knowing about it.

Never taking her eyes from the psi, Salis asks Demi about his communication activity. "Has he already contacted they ship?"

"Yes and I've placed a block between the two."

"Good hopefully we'll be able to learn something when they try to communicate. I'll try to get the codes you'll need to answer any communications. You'll need to record the voice for answering so as not to alert them to what's going on down here."

"You'll have to get the information quickly or they will become suspicious if we block them for too long."

"I'll get them as fast as I can." Still with her eyes on the psi, Salis ports the bands into her hands and holds them up for him to see. Concentrating she calls on her inner fire and within seconds the bands bursts into flames and slowly begin to melt. She drops them to the ground where they continue to melt into a unrecognizable blob. Reaching out, she sends the psi the message that she wishes to meet with him without the Emorphas being present.

'All of this really doesn't concern them. We will do nothing more than talk. I'm sure you wouldn't want them to hear the things we have to discuss.'

'I have no problem with my friends hearing whatever it is that you have to say, but if it will set your mind to rest, I will bring only three with me and we will all be unarmed.'

'Very well. We will meet you in the town square at the center table in two hours.' She breaks off from him and they turn back to the ship.

Once their inside Demi takes Colt to the med-unit and does a complete medical scan. He receives antibiotics and vitamin injections to make up for his deficiency in those areas. His neuro scan comes out fine with a slight increase in his alpha patterns.

After his medical, Colt goes to take a shower and get cleaned up. Though he was allowed to clean himself during his imprisonment, he had never felt really clean. He stays in the shower for forty-five minutes before shutting it off and stepping out. Not bothering with a towel, he walks back into the bedroom and finds Salis there laying out his clothes. She looks up as he enters the room.

"Feeling better?"

"Yeah. I feel human again." He tells her smiling slightly and walking to stand in front of her. "I've really missed you love." He reaches up to caress her cheek, then pulls her into his arms for a deep kiss. As he's kissing her, he strips her clothes from her and then pulls her down onto the bed with him.

"Colt, we don't have time . . ."

"We'll make the time. I need you Salis, the burning has been driving me crazy for the past week." Kissing her again he moves over her. Reaching between them he finds her ready and quickly enters her.

However much they would both like this joining to last, within minutes they come into their release. Colt collapses to Salis' side and waits for his breathing and heartbeat to slow back to normal. Turning his head slightly, he smiles at her and she smiles back.

"Now we both need another shower." She scowls at him, but ruins it by giggling. "Demi is going to be saying 'I told you so' as soon as I walk out of here."

"How's her free thinking program been working out?" He asks pulling her up from the bed and leading her into the bathroom.

"It seems to be working really well, at least when she uses it. I think Stephen has been telling her some of the negatives of being a free thinking android."

They step into the sonic shower and Colt turns it on. A couple of minutes later they step out again. "Why would he do that? Both he and Sarah ran a full diagnostic and cleared the addition of the program."

They go into the bedroom and get dressed. "I know. I think the report we got on the Colin Five unit had him rechecking the data on free thinking. The Alvation government reported last month that almost two hundred of their people had been life-ended by the Colin Five before it was destroyed."

"Surely they don't blame the free thinking program for that mess? Never in the history of androids having free thinking, has there ever been such a thing." He tells her pulling on his boots.

"I know, and I've pointed that out to both Stephen and Demi. I believe that the cause and the blame for what happened is the Colin units creators." She pulls on her vest and turns to face him. "Two weeks before the killing started, Kodar Temtei recalled the Colin Five unit for reprogramming. That reprogramming was supposedly for the purpose of the unit being used in a mining exploration. When I went over the Colin Five's previous programming I saw that everything needed for such an assignment had already been in its memory for the past ten months or so."

"Then why the recall and reprogramming?"

"I think that Temtei used the recall to cover up a plan to program the Colin unit to life-end either one or several people." Salis informs him as they leave the room. "Though I can't prove it yet, I'm sure that if the names of the dead are checked, we'll find some connection with Temtei."

"Why don't you have Stephen and Demi check it out when we get home? Maybe it will help to calm their circuits about the programming." He suggests as they walk through the ship. "If they find the proof on their own there's no way that they can deny that it wasn't the Colin unit's fault. His free will had been taken away."

Salis considers it as they near the ship's lounge. "That might work, but I'll have to get them clearance to look at the reports and his memory programs. After the murders all androids were restricted from seeing such things. The authorities are concerned that it might affect them in some way."

Colt frowns at this. "The only way that could happen is if something was embedded in the programs or reports to override their basic programming."

"We'll just have to wait and see. In the meantime, I've set out something for us to eat before this meeting." Salis tells him leading the way into the lounge.

Colt grins when he sees the array of food set out on the table. "Fine by me. I was wondering when I'd get some decent food." He sits down at the table and loads up his plate. They eat in silence and wait for Stephen and Demi so that they could make their plans for the meeting with the Federation psi.

Returning to his house after giving the Emorphas orders to keep a close eye on the ship, Japhet Trei attempts to contact the patrol ship again which is waiting on the dark side of the system. He tries for several minutes and then gives up in frustration.

At the first surge of power from his comm-unit Demi starts blocking the signal. To prevent him from knowing that they are responsible, she creates a static that resembles the effects caused by solar flares.

Turning to his personal computer unit, Trei makes out his report. "Though my plan to capture the Calidonian Princess was a success, she managed to escape with Blackwood and removed the blocking bands and destroyed them somehow, I will have to use a psi disrupter mechanism to neutralize their abilities. Once I have them under control again I will attempt to contact the Captain again. Solar flares have blocked communications again so it may be a couple of hours or a couple of days before I am able to reach the ship, though they are not expecting another contact for another week

"Two others arrived with the Princess. From their non-reaction, it is my conclusion that they are both androids. If this is the case they will have to be destroyed at the soonest possible time. The male unit is an older model, but the female unit is of a model I have never seen before. I believe that we should examine it closely to see what if any improvements it has before finally destroying it.

"I will have one of the female Emorphas simulate the Princess and see how well it will work on Colt Blackwood. The only problem that I can foresee will be simulating the Princess' psi abilities. As I reported earlier, I was unable to get any information from Blackwood as to the Princess' psi level or those of any of the Telepathic Alliance Council members. I was also still unable to gage Blackwood's psi level before the blocking band was destroyed. As near as I can figure he is between a five and a seven. I will attempt to get the information needed from the Princess before the patrol ship arrives in a week to take them to our base on Manglora." Ending his report he stands and walks over to the window.

He looks out at the Calidonian ship and frowns. Deep in the back of his mind, Japhet Trei knows that what he's doing for the Federation is wrong, but his family has always been loyal to them. Besides, the Telepathic Alliance has been interfering in the Federation's business for far too long. They had gotten in the way of the Federation adding several telepathic planets to their group. The only reason they did this was they thought the people would be used and their gifts exploited. Though it was true that if a planet could not provide any natural resources to be exported, then the people were put into service to cover their membership. Not many planets refused because they knew that the Federation would protect them. That was of course unless they turned against their protectors.

Turning back to his desk, Trei pushes a button on one corner and within seconds two Emorhpa enter the room. "I want everyone out of sight of the town square, but alert to any possible danger. You two and Shayara will accompany me. None of you are to be armed. The others will be armed, but I want their weapons on stun only. If either the female or male are injured or killed someone will pay the price. Now go have the others take their places, we leave in half an hour."

The Emorphas nod and quickly leave the room. Trei tries the communicator again and curses when he hears nothing but static. Shutting it down, he checks the telepathic disrupter to be sure that it is in working order.

On the Federation patrol ship the communications officer approaches his captain. "Sir, Mr. Trei hasn't reported anything more on the capture of the Calidonian Princess as he said he would."

"Have you tried to contact him to see what the problem is?"

"Yes sir, with no luck. All I get is static that resembles solar flares, though our science officer assures me that he has seen no such activity to warrant such a thing since the last one."

The captain frowns and then pushes some buttons on his own console. After studying his monitor for several minutes, he gets up and walks over to the science station. "Could this interference be from a previous flare?"

"It could sir, but it is highly unlikely since we have had two communications with Mr. Trei since the last one a week and a half ago. It has to be something else causing it sir. Flares just don't last that long."

"All right. I want a complete systems diagnostics done on both the communications and science stations. If everything checks out we'll go and check on Trei, though he did say to give him a week to work on the Princess. How long will it take for you both to do that?" The captain asks looking at each of the officers.

"Communications will take about eight to twelve hours for a complete systems check and diagnostic sir. I will have to do most of it myself since none of my staff has any experience with this new system yet."

"The science station will take twice as long because we'll have to check all of the sensor arrays as well."

"Very well, get started. Make it as fast as possible people or we'll have to wait for the next communication time and hope that everything is all right on the planet. Unless he misses two scheduled reports we can't approach the planet." The captain says and returns to his seat. He would be glad when this assignment was over and they could get back to some real duty.

CHAPTER 11

Demi's ship self continues to monitor the area around the ship and the meeting area, carefully noting and recording each of the positions taken up by the Emorphas around the meeting area. She also makes note of the weapons they have and the power signature. She has also had to block four communication attempts between the Federation psi and the patrol ship. All of this information is automatically transferred to her android self, who passes it on to Salis and Colt. "We need his codes and a voice print as soon as possible Salis. I've had to block three attempts from the psi and one from the patrol ship. The psi won't know what's happening, he'll just think that it's solar flares, but the ship may decide to investigate if I block them again."

"Isn't there another way to block the ship that won't draw their attention?" Colt asks frowning thinking that there had to be something that they could do to buy them more time.

"I could follow their signal back and attempt to create an internal problem, but chances are good that they're even now doing a diagnostic on their systems." She assures him.

"We'll do what we can to get what you need Demi. You can record his voice during the meeting and I'll try to 'see' the codes without him noticing. Though if he's any good he probably will notice so be prepared."

Stephen hands Salis and Colt psi enhancers to use in case there are any attempts made to block their abilities, which is a likely possibility. The enhancers are placed just beneath the surface of the skin at the temples, base of the skull, and the crown of the head. Once they're in place, Stephen turns them on and sets their output to a high enough setting that even a large psi disrupter will have little to no effect on them. He adjusts the settings slowly to give them time to adapt to the stimulation without overloading their brains.

After taking care of Salis and Colt, Stephen modifies both his and Demi's shields to ten times their normal strengths. At that intensity they will be able to withstand over a dozen blaster hits with no problem. While doing that he also strengthens their taser strength and distance.

Salis and Colt go over what they should ask and how they should ask. They don't want to give too much away, but the only way to get anything was to give him something, they want to find out as much as possible, as quickly as possible. "The first thing we need to find out is who he is and why he had you taken." Salis says looking at Colt. "There were three ships that left before you, which had only one or two people on board. Why didn't they take one of them?"

"They may not have arrived until I left, or the others may not have crossed their path. There's no way that they could have known when I would be leaving Calidon."

"Unless they have a spy on Calidon that is feeding them information." Salis points out having thought that this was the most likely explanation for them being in the same area at the same time as him. "The odds that you were the target are strong. You're in constant contact with the royal families of at least three planets, your father is the Alliance's representative to the Federation. No doubt they figured they could get whatever information they wanted out of you and if not use you to control your father."

"If there is a spy, then they would know of our relationship. They could have grabbed me to get to you. I may not have been the primary target." Colt points out where her logic could naturally lead to once everything was considered and all other possibilities were eliminated. He was sure that this is the true reason he was taken. Most of the Federation Council members knew his father and knew that he would never compromise his honor nor would any of his children.

"All right, so we have two possible reasons for your abduction. How do we find that out without endangering ourselves or the Emorphas?" She asks him knowing that it is highly unlikely that the psi would just come out and tell them. "I doubt that he'll give us a straight answer to anything."

"Either way, it doesn't matter. They violated the agreement with the Alliance as well as several of their own laws when they took me by force, along with endangering a nonmember of the Federation or the

Alliance. Justice will be on our side no matter what happens here."

"Then we should just get him to talk about what he's done and what the Federation expects to gain by all of this." Salis says and Colt nods.

When the time finally comes to leave the ship, they walk slowly to the town square. On the way, they observe the people watching from behind windows and shop doors. Before leaving the ship, Salis had made sure that both Stephen and Demi understood that no matter what the Emorpha did, they were not to be harmed. As they approach the square, they see the psi and three Emorphas waiting at the table for them. There are two men and a woman. The woman is about the same size and build as Salis. The men are standing on either side of the psi, while the woman is standing directly behind him.

While they are still several feet away, Demi warns them that there is a high powered psi disrupter mechanism in the psi's pocket. "Your enhancers are strong enough to counter it's highest setting, which is an alpha four. Since you're both alpha threes, almost twos, the most it would have given you without the enhancers would be a very bad headache, and maybe made you a little sick to your stomach."

"So with the enhancers we don't have to worry about either of those?" Colt asks for confirmation.

"Right. The only thing you should feel is a slight tingling when the mechanism is activated."

As soon as they reach the table, but before they sit down, Salis asks the psi his name and the reason why he had taken Colt. Though she doesn't expect an answer, she is surprised when he tells them.

"I am Japhet Trei of Arboro Prime. My family has been in loyal service to the Federation for over five generations. We do as they tell us, with whatever they tell us, no questions asked." He informs them, looking from one to the other but ignoring Stephen and Demi. "What my superiors want, is to know how your Alliance is capable of finding all of these telepathic worlds? They also wish to know why you continue to add them to your Alliance when the original agreement was for the four original worlds. Nothing was ever said about your taking in other worlds."

"That is incorrect Mr. Trei." Salis informs him evenly. "The original agreement is that the Alliance shall include all planets that have full psi abilities. The Alliance shall not exclude planets that have both psi and normal populations where the psi population is equal to, or less than that of the normal population. All planets that have more than a seventy percent chance of becoming completely psi within fifty standard years after first approach, shall be automatically included in the Alliance group of planets unless the planet as a whole prefers to stay separate from all planetary governing bodies." She smiles at him slightly before looking at each of the Emorphas. Her next words are to them.

"It also states that the Federation shall inform the Alliance of any and all planets that it may come in contact with that has psi abilities or the ability of metamorphoses, to give the planet the choice of neutrality." She looks back at Trei. "From what I have seen and heard, and from what I know, the Federation has broken that agreement. They did not tell the Alliance of the Emorphas existence, and they deliberately and maliciously lied to the Emorphas about the Alliance and our policies to keep them from joining. They took away their right of free choice."

"The Emorpha were given the information that they needed to make their decision. No one spoke negatively about your people to them at any point in time." He assures them with a slimy little smile.

Colt knows that the other man is lying and doesn't care that they know he is. "Why didn't the Federation just ask the Alliance Council what they wanted to know and why they wanted to know it? If they had done so they would more than likely have gotten an answer through proper channels. By allowing this action to take place against our people, we will have no choice but to consider it as an act of war."

"Your people cannot declare war against the Federation Mr. Blackwood. When you were taken there were no Federation ships present. There weren't even any Federation representatives near when you were taken." Trei reminds them adding, "The Princess came here of her own free will. It was her decision to look for and find you. Though I'm still not sure how she was able to locate you so quickly." He says frowning. It still bothered him that she had found him. After the cruiser had been destroyed any traces of its destruction had been removed.

"You still haven't answered our question as to why you had them take Colt. There were several ships that had left Calidon before him and passed through the same sector of space. Why wasn't one of them taken?" Salis asks a little more strongly.

Trei looks at her for several seconds before answering. "There was no premeditation in his being the one taken Princess. It was pure luck on our part that he was the one coming through at the time."

"What's your purpose in all of this Trei? What do you think we can do?" Colt asks frowning at the older man.

"I'm the one that is to get the information and asks the questions needed to get what we want. You can answer those questions and save me the time of looking for someone else to question. I will do anything necessary to reach the goal that has been set for me."

After almost an hour of listening to Japhet Trei talk in circles, asking them questions that the Federations council could have asked themselves through the proper channels, Salis finally calls a halt since it was getting them nowhere and she was starting to get a headache.

"Mr. Trei, no matter what you say or how you say it, we can't tell you what you want to know. The council and only the council can answer your questions. Neither of us are members of the council and therefore not qualified to do so." Salis tells him with a sigh over the wasted time, and stands up in preparation of leaving. "We have nothing further to talk about and since we have Colt back, we will be leaving and returning home. I'd advise you to call your superiors and inform them to contact the Alliance council for any answers they may want and to discuss what has happened and what can be done to rectify the situation that has been brought about."

Trei stands up slowly watching them closely. "Since you refuse to give me the answers I need, you leave me no other choice then to take the information I need." He quickly moves his hand into his pocket.

Knowing that he is switching on the psi disrupter, Salis and Colt flinch slightly as the tingling begins. Seeing them flinch, Trei orders the Emorphas to attack thinking that they are now psi disabled and no longer any threat to them. "Destroy the androids and take the Princess and Mr. Blackwood into custody. They can do nothing to stop you and I am tired of playing this game with them."

Before the Emorphas can make a move, Stephen and Demi stun the three with Trei and then turn to deal with the others while Salis and Colt deal with Japhet Trei. He is caught completely by surprise when he feels the psi energy directed at him. Even though he puts up a shield to protect himself, within minutes he is over powered and rendered unconscious. Once he's unconscious and collapsed over the table, the Emorphas immediately stop their attack. For several moments they just stand there looking confused and uncertain. Looking at each other they drop their weapons and start walking around and away from the square.

Colt reaches into Trei's pocket and pulls the psi disrupter from his pocket and turns it off. After looking at Salis, he uses his kinetic abilities to smash the mechanism and reduce it to a fine powder. While he's doing that, Demi and Stephen pick up the two males to carry back to the ship. Salis studies the female and then ports her to the ship.

After dusting off his hands Colt turns to Salis who is looking down at Trei. He flips the other man over and lifts his eye lids for Salis to make better contact with his mind. Salis reaches in and carefully takes the codes and information they need and sends it to Demi as they all return to the ship.

An hour later Japhet Trei regains consciousness and finds himself aboard the Calidonian ship. At first he is only able to move his head and look around his surroundings. When he tries to use his abilities to port himself off the ship he discovers that they aren't working. Sitting up slowly he closes his eyes and attempts to contact Shayara. When it feels as though his mind is on fire and shards of glass are being driven into him, he stops trying and opens his eyes again rubbing his temples to stop the throbbing. He couldn't believe that they had gotten through his shields so easily. When he was released he would strengthen them with an electronic enhancer.

Colt stands in the doorway of the holding cell and watches the other man attempt to use his abilities to no avail. He finally tells him "Your abilities have been temporarily neutralized. Until we know exactly what you've done to the Emorphas and how to correct it, your abilities will be of no use to you."

"You have no right to hold me here Blackwood. I am a member of the Galactic Federation of Planets and a free citizen."

"I remember saying just about the same words to you when it was you in charge Trei. Just as you ignored my affiliation to my Alliance, I shall ignore you yours." He nods to him and then leaves him.

During this time Salis and the androids are examining the Emorphas trying to find out how Japhet Trei was able to control them. Since he was controlling their minds, they needed to find out how long he had been in control, and what, if anything he used to gain and maintain that control. Once they know that, they must figure out how to return them to their normal state of consciousness and emotion.

"You're going to have to probe their minds Salis. Without anything specific for the med unit to identify, it can't identify any irregularities."

"I'd prefer doing it with their permission Stephen. With Trei it was different, I know what his response would be to our request for his codes or even to try and help him. Besides that he's an enemy to the Alliance and would have done the same thing if given the chance or the choice." Salis looks at each of the Emorphas laying out in front of her. "From what I know of these people, just from observation, I can't see them as our enemies."

"But it's the only way to get the information Salis." Demi points out looking up from where she is once again studying the Emorphas Federation medical files. "We can't take the chance of waking them to ask their permission. It's the only way for us to find out what we're truly dealing with. If their personalities are as we suppose, then I don't think that they will mind since it will help to free their people from whatever hold is over them."

Deciding that Demi is right, Salis carefully probes each of the Emorphas minds looking for a common thought or emotion that will give them what they are looking for. She finds that Japhet has had control of them for almost a year, but it isn't as strong as they had first thought, or as complete. His control of them is only superficial. Because there is such a large population a mind control drug was used to initialize control. Twenty were given the drug first, and then those gave the drug to forty more, until the whole population was under its influence. Japhet Trei then placed the suggestion that he was their friend and the Telepathic Alliance was their enemy. The only ones they could trust with their people's safety was the Federation.

"They were given some type of mind control drug about ten months ago. They have no idea what it was, but it was given by injection. The entire population was injected within two weeks."

"So what we're looking for is a possible psi inhibitor with a controlling agent." Demi says aloud still looking at her monitor. She goes through the files again examining the sections that show were injections were given. "Found it. They were given the suppressant and controlling agent in the guise of a mineral injection. It's one that will last two years and by then the subject is easy to control without the drug." Demi studies the files even closer. "He has to give them injections every five months to support the initial injection so that would mean that the drug should be at its weakest right now."

"Can you come up with something to counter the suppressant and agent?" Colt asks making his presence known to them.

Demi looks at him and then goes back to her monitor. "I'll see what I can come up with, but it may take me a while. Why don't you two go and get something to eat. I'll let you know as soon as I come up with something that we can use and that will work fairly quickly." She tells them working quickly at her console.

"What about these three, should we transfer them to holding rooms before they wake up?" Salis ask her looking at each of the Emorphas.

"Leave them here. I'll keep them sedated until I've come up with something to reverse their present state." Demi tells her never looking up from the screen.

〜

Thayer is in his ship board office thinking about Salis when the chime goes off indicating someone wanting to come in. "Enter."

"Majesty. We've reached the midpoint. Should we increase speed now or continue at our present speed?"

"Continue at present speed Lieutenant. Until we hear from the Princess on her situation we will act accordingly. I don't want to take the chance of having them attacked before we're in range to assist."

The Lieutenant bows and leaves Thayer to himself. After the door closes behind him, Thayer leans back in his chair and closes his eyes. He reaches out to Christa.

'Christa, have you heard from your sister again?'

'No Daddy, nothing yet. She's okay though, nothing's happened to her or Colt.'

'Let me know the minute you do sweetheart. If you get even the slightest inkling that she's in danger, I want you to let me know immediately.'

'I will Daddy. Don't worry, she'll be all right. Lissa wouldn't do anything to hurt herself or anybody else. Colt would only do what's necessary to protect her and any innocents that are with them.'

'I know baby. Kiss your mother and baby brother for me. Good rest.' He opens his eyes and stretches thinking to himself that he should have brought along one of the personal android trainers that Stephen had designed for him last year. He could use a good work out right now to deal with the stress of not knowing what was happening with his oldest daughter and her chosen mate. If anything happened to them the Federation

would wish to turn back the hands of time to change their decision to attack one of his children.

Demi goes through her chemical files looking for the right components that will stimulate the psi center and neutralize the inhibitor. It takes her a few hours to find the right combinations, but finally she does it. They would have to place it in the food or water for quick consumption or absorption. Both are ideal for what they need since it would get into the body quicker. It would be better still if they could inject the stimulator, but it would also take more time. Once introduced to the body it would take at least twelve hours to begin working, and at least another twelve before they would return to normal.

When Salis and Colt return, Demi explains how everything will work. "You will have to remove all directives placed by Japhet Trei. It would be easier if we could get him to do it himself, but the two of you can do it just as well. If the directives were not removed they would remain and possibly influence their actions without them knowing it."

"Do we remove the directives before or after the stimulator is given?"

"After Colt. With the stimulator in their systems it will help in the removal." Demi explains.

"Why not have Trei remove the directives himself? He's already got the connection with them and he could do it quicker." Salis points out. "We could control him while he does it to be sure that he doesn't do anything else."

"True, but it would mean you would have to be in a constant link with him until we were sure that every Emorpha has had the directives removed. We could use a controlling agent on him but that could prove dangerous to his mind because he would fight it." Demi explains knowing that Salis would not want the man harmed even though he was an enemy.

"How long will it take Colt and I to remove the directives from the entire population?"

Demi stands and walks over to where the Emorphas are lying still unconscious. "I'll be better able to calculate the time needed after you do these three. At this time I've calculated that it should take you the initial forty-eight hours to do the entire population. I gave these three an injection forty-five minutes ago. Why don't you both try the removal and see how easy it will make it for you. I'll time the process and then be able to tell you for certain how long it will take to do everyone else."

Salis does the woman, while Colt does one of the males. They both notice that the initial contact is much easier with the stimulator in their systems. Carefully they follow the pathways to the subconscious mind and feel for the unusual thought patterns. When they have located those patterns they carefully dismantle them until nothing of them remains. They carefully study every aspect of their brain patterns to be sure that they will understand the workings of the other minds they would be working on. After finishing the first two they work together on the other male and notice that it is even easier and quicker when they work together.

"You were right Demi, the stimulator did make it easier to reach their subconscious. We shouldn't have any trouble dealing with the others. How many do you think that we can handle at one time without endangering ourselves or the Emorphas?"

"With you working together I'd say no more than forty in an hour. If you take a rest every fifth hour you should have no ill effects. Though I think that we should be able to get some of the Emorphas to help out once they recover and things will go much faster. Since they know their own people they would be able to go in and get the job done in even less time. It is something that you should consider."

Both Salis and Colt do consider using the Emorphas to finish more quickly. They didn't want to waste any time getting the people back to normal. "How do you plan to introduce the stimulator to the rest of the people? We can't give them all injections."

"By the water. It will be the fastest way to introduce it to the population." Stephen explains agreeing that they could not give the whole population injections. "We'll go out tonight and place the stimulator into the water supply. By noon tomorrow they will all have some of the stimulator going through their systems through both ingestion and absorption. We should be able to notice when it begins to take hold and that will be the time for you to begin removing Trei's directives."

Later that night after they are sure that everyone is asleep, Demi and Stephen go out to place the serum into the water supply. Even though the Emorpha population is only a little over sixteen hundred people, they have split into four groups with four separate water supply tanks. To be sure that the serum doesn't become too diluted, Demi makes it into a strong concentrate that will permeate every water particle guarantying that a strong enough dose will be ingested or absorbed by everyone. Though it's strong, there would be no harm in them ingesting or absorbing large amounts. In fact the more they took in the faster it would work.

On the ship, Demi's other-self picks up the Federation's patrol ship on the long range scanners, headed towards the planet. Though Salis and Colt were asleep, this was something that needed their immediate attention.

"At their current course and speed they should reach the planet in four days."

"So they're not rushing to get here?"

"No Colt. It appears as though they are traveling on impulse power. They may not realize what has happened and are traveling slowly to give Japhet Trei time to contact them again."

"Have you had any luck in reproducing his voice patterns?" Salis wants to know, if not they were going to have trouble.

"Not enough to pass their analyses. I'm having trouble with his inflections."

"Then we'll have to take temporary control of his mind to communicate with them. The Emorphas won't be completely themselves until the day before the ship arrives. We have to do whatever we can to stall them and give the people the time they need to recover. We have to insure their safety." Salis tells them.

"How much should we control him though? If we control him too much his responses won't appear natural or normal, and if we don't control him enough he'll give us away for sure." Colt points out.

"I think that we should only control what he says to them and how he responds to their questions. We have to be sure that he doesn't give them too much information that could expose us, and not too little that would make them suspicious." Salis frowns wondering if they would be able to do that. She thinks about it for several seconds and then speaks to Demi. "Do we have any hypno drugs aboard? Could we use that along with our control to plant all the information we want him to relay?"

"It's possible, but the communication would have to be done quickly. I don't think that the drug would keep him under more than fifteen minutes." Demi tells her knowing how strong the man's mind was and how strong his beliefs in what he was doing. "The drug would have to be administered five minutes before the communication was setup so that he would be completely under and have no time to give a warning."

"All right then, we'll do that as soon as they get a little closer. We'll come up with an excuse for the delay in communication and try to send them back to wherever they've been hiding." Salis says covering up a yawn. "We'll go back to bed for a couple more hours. Wake us when it's time to start on the Emorphas." Her and Colt return to their room and fall almost instantly back to sleep.

When Demi and Stephen return from placing the stimulant, Demi tells Stephen that they can wake the Emorphas in the med center now. "Their biorhythms have remained the same for the past several hours now. I believe that they are back to their normal state of mind."

"Will they remember everything that's been said and done since the Federation took control of them?" Stephen asks as they head to the med center.

"Yes, they'll remember everything. The only thing removed were the directives, they should retain all memories of that time. There are no indications of any brain or nerve damage." She assures him as they enter the center. "I'll revive the woman first and then the men. From her reaction we should be able to gauge how the men will react when we bring them back to full consciousness thereby preventing a reaction we aren't prepared for." She administers a neuro stimulator and within seconds Shayara wakes and looks around her.

Blinking several times, Shayara looks at Demi and Stephen, then to either side of her at her companions Deinon and Naterion. "Where are we and why are Deinon and Naterion not awake?"

Demi steps slowly to her side so as not to frighten her and helps her to sit up on the examination table. "You are on the Calidonian Princess' Royal cruiser. Your friends are still unconscious for their safety as well as ours." She explains. After steadying the woman she steps back. "How do you think that your companions will react when we bring them out of their induced sleep?"

"As long as none of us is injured, they should remain calm. Our people are not normally aggressive unless something or someone threatens us. We believe that all life is precious and should not be harmed with few exceptions. As far as I know you have not harmed us or any of our people."

Nodding at her answer, Demi gives the neuro stimulator to the other two and steps back. As Deinon and Naterion wake and sit up, Shayara automatically mind links with them when she feels them beginning to morph. *'No brother. They have done us no harm and I do not believe that they ever have or plan too.'*

Both Deinon and Naterion look at Demi and Stephen, then back at Shayara. She notices that their eyes are still those of a predator ready to attack and defend. She is not sure what they have seen that she has not, but she still tries to control them.

"What have you seen that it makes you feel threatened to the point that you would change your form to attack?" When they start to answer by their mind link she shakes her head. "No, speak so that they can hear you." She tells them nodding to Demi and Stephen.

"They are not human, not alive, Shayara. They are machines, and we can't trust them as we would a human being." Naterion tells her with a growl.

"You are right. We are machines." Stephen confirms stepping slowly forward. "But our creators feel the same as your people. No life should be taken unless there is no other choice left. We are programmed with those beliefs and follow them."

Demi steps forward and stands beside Stephen. "My creator and her mate are resting. Shortly they will begin restoring your people to their proper mind set. They will remove Japhet Trei's directives so that your true beliefs will no longer be suppressed or in conflict with what you are doing."

The Emorphas look at each other and then probe each other to check. Before their minds touch they begin laughing. They have just realized that it is unnecessary. While under Japhet's control none of their people had been able to mind link with each other and Shayara had already done so without difficulty.

Demi and Stephen look at each other wondering what the Emorphas found so amusing. They wait until they have regained control and look to Shayara for an explanation.

"Please forgive our outburst. It only just hit us that I had done a mind link without even thinking about it."

"When Trei was controlling us, none of us could link with each other. The link was broken and made us easier for him to control." Deinon explains further. "Thank you for freeing us from his slavery."

"How can we ever repay you for what you have done for our people?" Naterion asks looking at each of them.

"Can you tell us how your people came to the attention of the Federation and what if anything you know of their plans regarding your people?" Stephen asks looking at each of them. "We need to know as much as possible to make an evaluation on the extent of their criminal actions, and intentions towards your people and others."

"We can't tell you much, for it is not our place to speak of such things." Naterion informs them. "All we can tell you is that, when some of our people returned home they acted strangely and no one could draw them into a mind link. Within what seemed like days, but was probably longer, everyone was affected even the children. I think the only ones to escape were the babies, but I can't be sure."

"As you probably know, our whole population consists of only sixteen hundred for the entire planet." Shayara says looking at Demi and Stephen and sees them nod. "That sixteen hundred is the last of our people as far as we know. That's as much as we can tell you. The elders will have to tell you the rest of our history."

"All right, we won't ask you anything else. Something we do need to know is if you can help my creator and her mate to help the rest of your people?" Demi asks watching them. "They could remove the directives themselves, but it would take them a long time to do everyone, and there is a Federation patrol ship headed this way. It would be best if all of your people were back to normal before they reach the planet so that we can plan how best to protect you."

Shayara looks at the other two unsure if they would be of any help. "We have never done anything like this before."

"If you were shown how, I believe that you would have no trouble." Stephen assures them. "Since you know the natural pathways of your people you could do them a lot easier then someone who does not."

"Can your people all link minds at the same time?" Demi asks coming up with another plan that might work even better and not leave so much strain on any of them.

"Yes, we use the link when we want everyone to know of something right away." Deinon tells them. "We also use it when someone needs help healing. With everyone linked together no one person is drained more than any other, and recovery is almost immediate."

Demi nods and looks at Stephen. "If Colt and Salis link with them and they link with their people I believe that the whole process can be done within six to eight hours Main if not faster. That would give us a few extra days for everyone to recover and for Salis and Colt to plan out our next step."

Stephen analyzes everything carefully considering all possibilities. They would still have to be sure that Colt and Salis rested for several hours afterward. Linking with people of a different mind pattern was draining no matter how long it was for. "It will work, but we have to discuss it with them first." He tells her and then looks at the Emorphas. "If you like we can give you rooms on the ship and you can meet Salis and Colt in the morning and discuss everything."

Naterion looks at his companions and then nods. "That would be fine. We will only need one room though. We are cousins and are fine with sharing a room."

"Very well. Demi will show you were you can rest while I secure the ship. If you would like something to eat she can show you to the galley." Stephen says and nods to Demi to show them the way.

CHAPTER 12

After meeting with Shayara and the men and agreeing that it would be better and easier to link with them to remove the directives from the other Emorphas, Salis and Colt practice linking their minds together so that it will seem more natural to them.

By mid-afternoon and over the next several hours they are all linked together and working to remove the directives from the minds of the Emorphas. It had been decided that to be in the center of the village would make the linkage even easier. After nearly five hours and though they are almost done, Salis and Colt collapse in mental exhaustion. Carefully Demi picks up Salis while Stephen picks up Colt.

Demi looks at Shayara. "Can you finish removing the directives? We have to sedate them so that their minds can rest."

Shayara nods looking at Salis and Colt with concern. “Yes, we watched how they did it and can finish. Will they be all right?”

“Yes. They just need to rest.” Demi assures them. “When you’re finished please come to the ship and we’ll give you some energy drinks to replenish you.” So saying she and Stephen carry their burdens back to the ship and undress them before placing them in bed. “Main, would you put cold compresses on their foreheads while I go and prepare re-energizing injections for them. I know that we need to get them back on their feet as quickly as possible, but I’d feel better if we let them rest for at least six to eight hours.”

“Then add a moderate sedative as well, otherwise they will be up in two or three hours.”

Demi nods and leaves the room, heading for the med center. She prepares the injections and then returns to the bedchamber. When she gives them the injections they stir slightly, but the sedative begins to work immediately and they settle back down into the comfort of the bed.

A couple of hours later Shayara and the others return to the ship and Demi gives them a re-energizing drink that also has a mild sedative and tells them to lay down for a while. “When you get up your people should be completely back to normal.”

Considering how tired they all feel they don’t argue with her, but drink their drinks and return to the room they had used the night before.

The Emorphas are just beginning to roam around checking on each other when the patrol ship attempts to contact Japhet Trei. Demi relays their communication through Trei's unit so that the Federation people won't know that they are now in control. Colt keeps a light touch on Trei and leads his answers carefully having quickly studied the other man's mind as the hypno drug started taking effect.

"I had a slight malfunction with the communicator and wasn't sure if you got my message not to approach until I have the ship secured. The Princess came with two androids that are free thinking. Until they are out of commission, it wouldn't be in our best interest for them to learn of your presence. They could still contact the Princess' people."

"We didn't receive your message. We were having problems with our unit as well. Though our comm officer couldn't find anything, this is the first free communication we've had since your last contact stating that you had captured the Princess. I think that it would be best if we came in and took control of the situation. We don't have much time left before her people come looking for her. We can block any of the ships attempts to contact her people."

"No Captain. They haven't detected you yet, but if they do they will send out a distress signal to alert the Alliance of our presence. It is my responsibility to get a replacement for the Princess and send it back to Calidon. If you show up now you jeopardize that mission." Colt stops there unsure if all of this information was true or not.

"Very well Trei. We'll return to our previous location and wait for your next scheduled communication. They won't be able to detect us."

"Thank you Captain, I'll contact you in the next four days to let you know what is happening. I should have everything set and in place by then."

"You had better Trei. Understand that you only have four days and then we come in and take over."

The communication is ended and Colt releases Trei's mind. Stephen then takes the other man back to the holding cell while Colt drinks a psi booster. Soon Salis and Colt would have to go and meet with the Emorpha leaders. He just hoped that they would find a solution to all of this before there was any more trouble and someone ended up hurt or worse.

At the meeting with the elders they learn the history of the Emorphas. Each of the elders tells a small part of the history as they know it, but before they begin they apologize to Salis and Colt for what has happened.

"Your Highness. On behalf of our people we would like to apologize for all that you have been put through. It is not our way to harm or detain people in any way." Belina bows her head to Salis.

"Please don't apologize Belina. None of what has happened is your peoples fault. You were being controlled by another and we hold him and the ones he works for responsible for all that has happened." Salis assures her both vocally and telepathically. "You were being used as so many others have been in the past."

Belina and the others nod their heads in thanks for her understanding, sure that many others would not have been so forgiving or understanding. Then Dengarlee the eldest of them starts the tale of their history.

"Two thousand years ago our number was nearly a million strong. Many felt a pull to leave our home over a thousand year period. This exodus brought us down to about two hundred and fifty thousand. Then our people began to change. Not all at once, but a few hundred at a time. Each new birth the changes came more and more pronounced and noticeable until it was in all of us. Some of the people couldn't handle the changes and went mad. They started killing others and then themselves. Even some of the children were murdered by these people. This went on and off for nearly three hundred years until our numbers were cut by over half. Those that didn't die and were still disturbed, several thousand, left thinking that if they were no longer here they would return to normal." Dengarlee tells them, and then Keley takes up the story.

"After all of this, the ones left embraced the changes and began taking on other forms. Mostly for entertainment, but it was also to see what we could now do. Many of the people became so enmeshed in the forms they had taken to the point that most chose their favorite ones and stayed in those forms permanently. We figure that after a while they must have forgotten how to change back and became forever locked into their new forms. Most of the animals on the planet are tied to us in some way or another."

"If they became animals and are still connected to you, how do you keep from killing them?" Demi asks because this statement is not logical to her. "Your people eat meat and protect your farm animals from predators. You would have to kill to protect your livestock and yourselves from attack. How do you know which animals are connected to you and which are not?"

"We can feel the connection and so can they. There has never been a time that any one has killed a changed one by mistake. Every once in a while we may have to end one's life that becomes a threat to the people through madness or disease, but for the most part they and their offspring remain in the wilds."

"There have been occasions when they have brought us young that were born either human, or shortly after birth became human. These children are very special to us because they mean that certain family lines will survive another generation. We know though that for many they will only have offspring that are completely animal. There is no doubt that we have probably taken the lives of those who's ancestor was originally one of us, but the bloodline is so diluted by animal genes they no longer touch us. That's why whenever we take any animals life we ask their forgiveness and thank them for contributing to the continuation of our people. " Belina tells them with a small smile.

"But knowing what can happen when you change form, you still do so. What keeps you from staying in those forms?" Colt asks wondering how they could control such a thing especially when in animal form.

"When the population got down to about fifteen thousand, it was decided that a safety would be placed deep within everyone's subconscious. If anyone holds another form for three months without changing back to their true selves at least once each month, the safety does it automatically. After that they won't be able to change again for at least a year." Keley tells him.

"Did Japhet or anyone else know of this safety mechanism?" Salis asks wondering what the chances of the Federation knowing and their probable reaction.

"It's unlikely. No one would have told him and there would be no way for it to be removed or altered. It was first introduced a couple hundred years ago and has become a natural part of all of us. It no longer has to be implanted, everyone is born with it."

"So even if the Federation wanted you to replace someone, you couldn't do it for a long time without discovery. Either by changing back every so often or by going the three months and automatically changing back to your true forms." Salis concludes.

"Yes, and though he had control, we still had our own thoughts. We just couldn't speak them or share them with our people." Dengarlee tells them. "About twenty-five years ago some of our people decided to use our abilities to entertain others. We had been receiving images of plays and dances for quite some time and started mimicking what we saw. We took on the forms we saw and became the characters of the play or dance. Because of our ability to change form, we could become anyone or anything. We can also pick up speech patterns and mannerisms.

"The ones that had learned quickly were the first of the Brightstar acting group. They went to different planets and performed plays and musicals to the delight of their audiences. People would bring scripts and ask if the group would perform them, or show them videos of old performances and ask them to do those. There were some that had old family diaries, and wanted to have what was written down performed so that they could see what their ancestors might have looked like and how they may have lived."

"With our peoples ability to change into another form, be it human or animal, just looking at a picture or even getting a very good description enables us to take on that form." Keley explains some of the things they do. "There are also many of us that can touch someone or something and take its physical form on completely. Every detail is picked up from that touch and it is hard to tell which one is the copy and which is the original. Even the smallest physical detail is taken on. This is what made our acting troupe so popular. For some they even take on the brain pattern of the individual that they have touched. Though we have never shared that bit of information with anyone."

"Then about eighteen months ago the troupe was approached by a Federation spokesman and asked to perform for some of the leaders. It was thought that such a performance would be good for our people so it was agreed that a performance would be given. Belina's daughter Shayara was part of the troupe, as was Keley's son Naterion, and my grandson Deinon. We lost contact with them but did not worry because it had happened many times before. When they returned home almost eleven months ago though we knew that something was wrong because we still couldn't touch their minds. Before we could do anything, we were all drugged and under the control of Japhet Trei."

"He told us that we were needed to help the Federation gain control of some planets that were a threat to the safety and wellbeing of all the known worlds." Keley informs them. "He then proceeded to tell us how your people were going from planet to planet enslaving those with lesser or no abilities than your own. He showed us pictures of what he said were the atrocities done by your Alliance and that it would happen to us too if you should find us."

"Though deep in our subconscious we knew that this was not true because we had already heard about your people, our conscious minds accepted it as the truth."

Belina says looking from Salis to Colt. "Then about five months ago, he started telling us that we had to capture one of the leaders or a member of their family and replace them with one of our people. When that person had enough physical evidence that your Alliance was corrupt, they could move in and take over and then our people would be safe. About six weeks ago Japhet heard that Colt was leaving Calidon to join you on Manchon until it was time for you to return to Calidon for your lifemating." Belina stops when Colt scowls deeply and curses.

"So they do have a spy on Calidon. Damn." Colt swears again and looks at Salis. "They probably know that Thayer's on his way here now and have an armada headed for us. We need to warn him and have him bring re-enforcements."

Salis nods and closes her eyes and concentrates on Christa. It would be better if she could lay down but they didn't have time. *'Where's father now Ista?'*

'He's still about two weeks away from you. He's traveling at normal speed to give you the time you asked for.'

'If he travels at maximum speed how long before he could reach us?'

'About five or six days. Do you want him to go that fast?'

'Yes. Faster if possible. Tell him to keep a look out for a Federation armada headed this way. There will probably be one out there. Don't say anything to anyone except mother about this. Colt and I believe that there is a spy in the palace that may have already warned the Federation of father traveling this way.'

'I'll tell him and warn Momma.' There is a slight pause. *'Momma says to take care and that she wishes she could be there with you.'*

'I know. Tell her not to worry just take care of our baby brother. Father can handle things when he gets here. We've got all the proof we need against the Federation for ourselves and the Emorphas.'

'Momma will still worry until you're home but I'll tell her. We love you Lissa.'

'I love you too Ista. Be good and be safe.' Salis opens her eyes and gives her head a little shake. It was still so strange that she could talk with Christa from such a long distance but not their parents. "Christa is telling father now. She'll warn him to watch for the Federation ships and to come as fast as he can. She figures he should get here within five days to a week."

"Let's just hope that Thayer reaches us before the Federation does." Colt warns her and for several moments they all just sit there and stare at each other knowing that if the Federation reaches them first, their chances of holding them off until help arrived was slim to none.

Back at the ship Stephen goes over the ships systems with Demi's ship self to make sure that everything from the weapons to the shield generators were in working order. He wants to be sure that there is no possibility of a mishap should they be placed under attack by the Federation. They would have to talk with the Emorpha about bringing the children and possibly the elderly on board should there be an attack. Even though the population was quite small, and the ship a reasonable size, there just wasn't enough room for everyone. If the Emorpha had some place that they could all gather, he could put together a shield to protect the people that couldn't get on the ship, but they would have the protection of a ship's shielding.

"Main, all my shields and weapons have been fortified two hundred percent. The only way we could sustain damage now would be a direct hit by a dozen blast cannons in the same location at the same time." Demi's ship-self assures him with some pride.

"We will need to set up a generator to create the same shielding for any Emorpha that can't get on the ship."

"I have an extra shield generator in my cargo supply hold that we can use. It won't take much to modify it to the same specifications." She tells him remembering the generator Salis had put on board wanting to have a replacement just in case. "From everything that Salis and Colt have learned, there is no way that the Federation could know that the Emorphas wouldn't be able to deceive anyone for longer than three months. There's a safety in their minds that prevents them from holding an image longer than that."

"We would have a better case for the Emorpha as well as ourselves if we knew who had sent Japhet Trei on this mission and who the spy on Calidon is." Stephen says with a frown.

"I've had my systems checking Trei out since we learned his name, but so far I've only run into dead ends. Every time I think that I've found his master it turns up he was only on loan from someone else. It goes on like that for the past fifteen years."

"Run checks on any that are repeated more than fifteen times. Check the time periods between those repeats and look for a pattern. His true master is in there. Cross reference with family members to show any possible links. Whomever is controlling him would keep close tabs on his whole family and he would return to that person on a regular basis.

When Salis and Colt finally break eye contact, Colt turns to the others. "Is there one of your men that would be willing to take on Japhet Trei's form for a little while?" He asks looking at each of them. "The patrol ship is nearby and others are probably on their way. It's too hard to control Trei without taking the chance that they'll pick up on his struggle to warn them."

"We will have to ask around, but we should be able to find someone that can and will take his place for you." Keley assures them.

"Will your Alliance accept us when this is all over your Highness?" Dengarlee asks knowing that they would need the protection of others after this.

"Please, call me Salis and yes you will be accepted into the Alliance. Though most of the planets in the Alliance are made up of telepaths, you would qualify as well. You have telepathic abilities that aren't very strong, but you do have them. Even if you didn't have any telepaths there would be the strong possibility of your being accepted on your morphic abilities alone and your need for protection. The Alliance would never leave you unprotected after what you've already been put through. None of our leaders condone slavery of any kind, but especially the kind that uses a peoples abilities to control or harm others."

"If you join the Alliance the different planet members would send some of their people to live here. Your people too would have to select some to travel to the other planets as well. We do this so that everyone in the Alliance can learn from each other and become more supportive." Colt explains to them the basics of the Alliance. "The people that participate are encouraged to find lifemates if they are not already mated. It could also help to build your population back up."

"What exactly is this lifemating?" Keley asks with a slight frown.

"A lifemating is done when two people are interconnected. When they feel as one even though they are not touching." Salis tries to explain. "For most people that are meant to be together, there is what we call a burning. It starts out with only a tingling, but then becomes stronger and stronger. The two need contact at times to stop the pain of the need they feel. When their time for the lifemating is right, the burning will be constant and they must be in constant physical and mental touch until their mating ceremony. When they are lifemated they become as one. One in body, mind, and spirit. Forever linked to each other."

Keley nods and looks at Belina and Dengarlee. *'As our soul mates are. Maybe with this Alliance our young people will find the other halves of themselves.'* "We understand your lifemating now. It is much like our soul mates. We would be honored if such were to occur between our people and yours Salis."

Colt then goes on to explain what would be expected of them as members of the Alliance. "No one member can commit the whole of the Alliance to an assault on anyone without just cause. If the Alliance as a whole decides that action must be taken, then it is done with little or no loss of life if at all possible. We prefer to save lives rather than take them."

"I came on my own because I had no proof that the Federation was involved." Salis admits to them. "I went against the wishes of my grandmother and will be punished accordingly. That will happen to anyone who acts on their own under the same conditions."

"You will still be punished even though you have proved that there was just cause for your actions?" Belina asks frowning in disbelief.

"Yes. You must agree that what I did was very foolish Belina. Not only did I endanger my own life and safety, but those of every member of the Alliance. If something had gone wrong before I had the proof needed, there is no way that the Alliance could have known what was happening and people would have suffered. I will gladly take what the Alliance considers just punishment for my actions." She looks at each of them. "Will your people be able to accept such if it is them that endangers others?"

"We would hope that they would be as honorable and as willing." Dengarlee admits.

"Don't think that it will be a harsh punishment. No one is ever punished more than is deserved." Colt assures them seeing and sensing their uncertainty. "All evidence is recorded and logged so that a fair judgment can be made in all cases. When the ending justifies the beginning it all comes out fairly."

"All right, that sounds fair enough." Dengarlee agrees. "But what does your Alliance get from us when we join? Our planet has no special qualities, nothing that would benefit anyone else. Will they try to use our abilities as the Federation had planned to use them?"

Belina gasps at his words. "Den! That was uncalled for." She admonishes him embarrassed that he would say such a thing after all that Salis and Colt had done for them.

"It's all right Belina. Dengarlee has a valid question." Salis assures the older woman and then looks at the older man. She lets him see the truth within her heart of hearts. "No one in the Telepathic Alliance would ever use your abilities in such a way. What the Alliance will get when you join us, to share in your knowledge, to know your friendship and loyalty, and to become as a family with you. The Alliance will share your joys and sorrows and help you to the best of its abilities for as long as the Great One wishes it for all of us."

Dengarlee continues to look into her eyes until he feels deep in his own heart, that her words and belief are true and solid. He nods and smiles apologetically. "Forgive me Salis, Colt, I had to be sure for our people, and for my own peace of mind."

"No apology needed Dengarlee. It was an honest question and concern that deserved an honest answer." Colt assures him and then shares a smile with Salis. Both had wondered when the question would be asked.

"I think that we have all learned what we needed to learn from each other." Keley states standing. "It's almost time for the evening meal. We've been discussing things all through the day. Will you join us?" He asks looking from one to the other. "It will give our people a chance to meet you and form their own opinions. We try to encourage everyone to make their own decisions and then discuss it with our council of elders if they have any concerns that are on their minds."

"We would be honored to join you and your people for the evening meal." Salis smiles at him as she stands and then looks at Demi. "Why don't you go back to the ship and help your father with the rest of the ship's check. We'll return in a few hours."

Demi nods and then leaves. Her humor circuit kicks in as she plays back the expressions on the Emorpha leaders faces when Salis said that she, Demi, had a father. She would have to replay the image for Stephen and see what his reaction was. He sometimes had a problem with Salis calling him her father and Sarah her mother.

Stepping out of the meeting house, Keley frowns as he watches the android walk away. As the others join him he turns to Salis. "You called the male android the female's father. How can you call it anything but what it is?"

Salis frowns for a second before understanding comes and laughing out loud. "Forgive me Keley. I wasn't laughing at you." She quickly explains as Keley starts to frown at her outburst. "Yes, both Stephen and Demi are androids, but their more than that. Stephen is Demi's father in much the same way that you are Naterion's. Where Naterion has your genetic make-up, Demi has Stephen's memory circuits and a few other 'genetic' parts." She explains as they begin walking to the communal meal house. "Stephen and his counterpart have been with my family since before my mother's birth. Demi was created from parts of both Stephen and Sarah, to become her own unique self. I'm afraid that sometimes I forget that they aren't human."

"I can see where you would." Belina admits. "Unless you look into it's . . . her, eyes, you would mistake her for a human female."

"That's what I was hoping for when I designed and built her. To me she's not just an android, but a friend and a part of the family. At times I still think of Stephen and Sarah as my special aunt and uncle."

"Is this Sarah also an android?" Keley asks opening the door to the meal house.

"No, Sarah's still only a console unit, but hopefully within the next year or two she'll have an android body as well."

All during the supper Salis and Colt tell them about their lives and their people. They hold nothing back, wanting to show the Emorpha that they trust them with their most treasured and emotional memories.

CHAPTER 13

Over the next few days Colt and Salis meet with the elders to plan out their deception against the Federation. The room is octagonal in shape, and there are paintings that depict the Emorpha's lives for many generations. The table and chairs look and feel well used and are well taken care of. The first day of their meeting Keley introduces them to Pariben Trencher who has agreed to take Japhet Trei's form for the deception.

"Pariben is one of our best shape holders. His detailing is very fine." Keley praises the young man causing him to redden in the face with embarrassment.

Colt looks Pariben over and then nods. "He has the same physical build as Trei, so the form won't be too difficult for him to hold. How much detail can you take from Trei that could pass a computer scan?"

Pariben frowns slightly not sure he understands. "Visually there would be no difference, or vocally for that matter. I can take his eye color and the shape of his retina down to the smallest blood vessel if necessary."

"What about his brain patterns? Would you be able to mimic those as well?" Colt asks with some concern. "I ask because there is a slight possibility that they could run a neuro scan while your speaking to them just to make sure that it is really him. No doubt the Captain is well aware of your people's ability to take on another's form."

Pariben frowns again and looks at his leaders. "I'm not sure if I can do that. There are only a few of us that have ever been able to do that, and those are mostly females." He looks back at Colt. "I'll be willing to give it a try if you want." Since his sister was one of the females it might be possible for him to do it as well.

Colt looks over to Salis. *'We should give it a try. If they run a scan they'll know that we've taken control down here.'*

'But how do we find out? We can't waste time on testing, we only have a couple of days before we have to contact them again.'

'We'll have him try it on one of us first. Demi can check him and let us know how good it is. She's more sophisticated than anything the Federation may have. Just a level three scan would get him past their system if he can pick up the pattern and hold it for ninety seconds.'

'All right, but it will have to be you. I've been having small energy surges since we woke up this morning.'

Colt frowns a little at her, concerned that something could be wrong. He then looks from Pariben to Keley and the others. "Pariben, we'd like you to give it a try right now if you don't mind? Demi will check to be sure that it gets past their scanners."

"Who should I try it on?" He asks, looking at everyone.

"Me." Colt tells him standing and walking a couple of paces away from the table. "Since I'm not one of you, it will be a more accurate test. Since your people all link together regularly, you can easily take each other's patterns without even knowing it." He explains.

"All right, but what do I have to do? As I said, it has ever only been females with the ability who have ever tried this before." He reminds them nervously also standing and going over to Colt.

Salis joins them and speaks calmly and softly to Pariben. "First try to link your mind with Colt's. He won't help you, you'll have to do it on your own." Pariben closes his eyes and tries to do as she says. When he can feel the link between them he smiles and nods never opening his eyes. Salis steps closer to him and speaks even softer into his ear, her voice almost hypnotic. "Now, slowly let your mind and his flow together. That's it. Flow with it until you feel that you are in perfect sync with him."

Stepping away, she walks over to Demi who has been scanning them since they began. After about five minutes she nods that they are sharing the same pattern. Salis walks back over to Pariben and once again speaks softly to him.

"Okay Pariben, now very slowly pull yourself out, but keep that flow in your mind for as long as you can." She watches him closely and waits. Every few seconds she looks over at Demi to confirm that he's still doing it and gets a positive response. "I want you to have a conversation with Dengarlee now. You have to keep that flow for at least ten minutes." Pariben frowns slightly but nods his understanding and Salis looks at Dengarlee. "Talk to him. Try to run him through as many emotions as you can to test his control."

For the next five minutes Dengarlee talks to Pariben, making him angry, sad, happy, and excited. At the end of the five minutes Salis calls a halt to the test. "You can let go of the pattern now." She tells Pariben and then looks at Demi for her analysis of how Pariben had done.

"It took him a while to get the pattern and he almost lost it when he pulled out, but he regained control almost immediately. The only time that the pattern shifted was in the moments of sadness, but not on any significant level that would put out an alert."

"So he could control the pattern well enough to get past one of their neuro scans?" Colt asks wanting to be absolutely sure before they tried this.

"I believe so Colt. He was also able to pick up on your Alpha waves, which I didn't think could be done." Demi confirms with a frown realizing that such a thing was dangerous to all telepaths and she would have to report it to Salis when they were away from the Emorphas. "What I scanned could easily have been your own brain patterns."

Colt nods and looks at Pariben. "Well, we know that you can do it. If you'll go with Demi to our ship, she'll put you where you can study Trei until its time. Either she or Stephen will get him to talk so that you can hear his speech patterns and get those down as well."

"Thank you sir. I hope that I can perform well for you when the time comes." Pariben bows to Colt and then Salis. He turns to face his leaders. "With your permission I'll go to their ship now."

Belina nods and raises her hand. "You will do well Pari. Have faith in yourself and you will always do well." Pariben nods to her and then turns and follows the android from the building.

After he leaves Belina and the others begin discussing what should be done if fighting should break out on the planet. None of their people really had any experience with fighting others since they were a peaceful people.

"Your Majesty. We've picked up at least two Battle Cruisers in our wake." Akanit Idolim reports looking up from his monitor. "They are PRC class ships."

Thayer steps over to the man's station to look at the monitor. He frowns and then nods. "Good job Akanit. How far behind us are they?"

"Approximately one, maybe two days at least Majesty."

"All right. Thank you. Inform the other ships if they haven't noticed them and tell their Captains to go to yellow alert. When we're a day out from Brightstar put all ships on red alert, unless there's a need to do it sooner." He looks down at the young man when he senses a spasm of fear. "Why don't you say an Aquilian prayer for guidance and strength? I think I could use all the help I can not to worry so much about the Princess."

"I will Majesty. I'll say one for all of us." Akanit assures him and then adds, "I'm sure the Princess is fine Majesty."

"Thank you Akanit." Thayer says patting his shoulder and then walks back to his office off the bridge. "Sarah, what can you tell me about those Cruisers?"

"They are crewed by an elite group of soldiers that are trained to do whatever is necessary to maintain order and control. If a hostile world does not comply when given the chance, they don't get another. They eradicate, secure, and maintain until otherwise ordered. No humanoid life is left when they're done."

"Even women and children?" He asks not wanting to believe that these men would follow such orders that would condemn women and children so arbitrarily.

"ALL humanoid life Thayer." Sarah confirms.

"Damn! How long have they been in use?"

"Five years, six months, eleven days. They have been used twice since the first day they were commissioned. Four years ago on Xanora III and again twenty-one months ago at Bemissara."

"But why use them on Brightstar? Though I don't condone the killing of women and children for any reason, those planets did have something evil about them at one point that drove telepaths almost catatonic. Brightstar is nothing like either of those planets. If it was neither Salis or Colt could stand the negativity." Thayer tries to rationalize what he has just learned.

"Did any telepath that you know ever confirm that evilness Thayer?" Sarah asks pointedly since they were talking about the Federation. "Any telepath from the Telepathic Alliance of Planets? No, no one. The only telepaths to set foot on either of those worlds were and are working for the Federation. I've been checking their telepaths since Salis sent us the name of the one they're having to deal with. They're all related in some way. My analysis of the information we have is that the PRC is being used to cover up failed takeover attempts by the

Federation, or more precisely a certain faction of the Federation."

Thayer considers this and then nods. He didn't believe that all of the leaders on the Federation Council could be involved. While he was undercover for them he had met the members at one time or another and could sense no malevolence in most of them. There had been a few that he had thought deserved watching. It wouldn't be a surprise if they were the ones involved in all of the problems with the Federation.

"So they know that something has gone wrong on Brightstar and are sending the PRC to see what it is. If it's not in their favor, they'll move in and kill everyone so that no one else will ever know about it."

"That's my analysis of the situation. Whoever ordered those ships expects trouble of some kind and doesn't want anyone left behind to tell about what was happening on Brightstar."

"How long before we reach Brightstar?"

"We'll be in orbit in less than four days. The cruisers will arrive within thirty-two point six five hours of our arrival. There won't be much time to prepare."

"I had better let Salis and Colt know what we'll be up against. They need to get the Emorphas ready for an attack. Contact the Captains of the other ships and have them transported over here for an emergency meeting. I want to at least have some kind of plan in place before we arrive." He sits back in his chair and closes his eyes to concentrate on Salis and Colt.

Federation battle cruiser PRC One bridge. A corporal slowly approaches his commanding officer and stands at attention. "Commander Olivinite, navigation says that we will reach the planet in six solar days. Scans have not picked up the Alliance ships as of yet but they are continuing to scan on all bands for any anomalies."

"Thank you corporal. Inform me when they pick up those ships."

"Yes Sir." The corporal turns to go and then turns back again. He didn't like informing on his fellow soldiers but the Commander deserved to know that some of the men were uneasy.

Commander Olivinite looks up when he realizes that the corporal was still there. "What is it Corporal?"

"Commander, I just thought that you should know that some of the men are uneasy about this mission. They question the wisdom of attacking this world if the Alliance is there to protect it. We know nothing about their ships or their mental capabilities." The Corporal swallows hard when the Commander begins to frown.

Scowling at the Corporal, Commander Olivinite looks around the bridge wondering who those men were. He was sure that the Corporal wouldn't give him any names. "What about you Corporal? Do you agree with those men?"

"No Sir. I do as I'm told without question for you and our Mistress."

"Good man. Return to your post." Olivinite waves him away still scowling. Tapping the arm of his seat for several minutes he finally pushes the ships intercom. "Attention all hands. It has been brought to my attention that some of you question our Mistress' orders. I may not have your names now, but I will and you will answer to me as well as our Mistress. We will not let a bunch of mutants dictate how we will do things. If they get in our way we will wipe them out like anyone else that goes against the Federation and or Mistress. I suggest that you rethink your present stand and decide whether or not you are PRC elite material or not. If not you will get your walking orders upon our return to Federation space and you will be expected to payout the rest of your service to the Federation and our Mistress. Anyone not able to do so will become permanent servants to the Mistress or anyone else she wishes to give you to along with your families. Think long and hard soldiers, you have until missions end to decide."

~

On Brightstar, Salis interrupts Dengarlee when she feels the touch of her father calling to her. She and Colt close their eyes to focus on hearing him.

'We can hear you father.'

'We'll be there in four days with six ships. You need to prepare for a serious fight sweetheart. There are two PRC Federation Battle Cruisers behind us that will arrive a little under thirty-six hours after us. According to Sarah they won't leave any witnesses.'

'Aren't they the ones that attacked Xanora and Bemissara?'

'Yes they are Colt. You need to get anyone that can't help in the fighting safely away from the villages, especially the women, children, and elderly. If at all possible we'll try to transport them up to the ships.'

'Would four of the ships be able to handle about four hundred people each? There are about that many in each

village and it would be better if we didn't separate them if we don't have to. Though many will want to stay and fight.'

'They can handle it. I hope that we won't have to use the ships during the fight. From what Sarah and I can figure out all of the fighting will take place on the planet. They wouldn't want any evidence in space to an unfair battle. If they can't get the situation under control they will kill everyone and then annex the planet and repopulate it later.'

'We'll get started right away father. Take care.'

'You too little one. Colt, watch out for my girl and yourself.'

'I will Thayer.'

Salis and Colt open their eyes and look at Belina and Dengarlee. "We need to find safe places for all the women, children, elderly, and anyone that can't bring themselves to fight." Salis tells them and then lets Colt explain what they had just learned.

"The men on these ships are trained to eradicate all humanoid life on a planet with no exceptions. They don't take prisoners and they have no mercy when it comes to women and children either. Everyone will die and the Federation will have a new planet to colonize."

"If these men are coming here to destroy us how can we stop them? Our people have never really fought before." Dengarlee tells them standing and pacing around the room. "Japhet had us training to be fighters and killers, but that goes against all that we know and believe in. I doubt that any of us will be of much use to you."

"We believe the same Dengarlee, but we also believe that if it's the difference between children living or dying, then our beliefs must take a sideline as far as their safety is concerned." Salis tells him softly. "What is more important to you Den? Your belief that all life deserves to live, or that children are to be protected above all others? Don't the children have the right to grow up as the Great One planned for them? Or should they take their chances in life like everyone else even though they are unequipped to protect themselves in most cases?" Though she doesn't mean to be so harsh, she wants the Emorpha to realize that to her people children will always come first. It doesn't lessen their belief in the Great One, but strengthens their bond with Him. They feel that if they were to do nothing to protect the children and the innocent, then they would be truly turning their backs on the Great One.

Dengarlee stops near Belina and she reaches out to touch his arm lightly. "She's right Den. The children are more important than some of our beliefs. The Great One teaches us that the children will lead us and must always be protected. If you must hold on to a belief, then hold on to that, and Him. Believe that He will not turn away from us if we do what we must to insure the survival of our children, if not ourselves."

Closing his eyes and sighing heavily because he knows that they are right, Dengarlee nods. "We will do what we must to protect our children." He opens his eyes and looks at Salis. Though she can see and feel his sadness and distress at what must be done, she can also see his determination to do whatever he must to insure their safety.

"All right, where can we send them or put them where they'll be safe, but where we can still protect them if they are found?" Colt asks getting everyone back to the matter at hand.

"Each village has a deep cave nearby where we store extra provisions in case we should have a bad year or a hard winter." Dengarlee tells him returning to his seat. "Each cave is capable of holding our entire population if necessary."

"That would work if we could get everyone here from the other villages. It would be best if we could keep the fighting in one area. I realize that this village could very well be destroyed, but I think that having everyone in the same place would also make it easier to evacuate should the need arise. Sarah could lock onto everyone and get them to the ships more quickly without having to probe several areas at the same time." Colt explains seeing the frowns on their faces. "Of course we would help you to rebuild should the village be destroyed. I hope that it won't come to that though. How far is the cave from the village?"

"They all vary, but this one is about three miles to the east of your ship." Belina answers.

"Do they have any type of shielding, even something that keeps animals out." Salis asks wondering if Stephen and Demi would have to rig up a shield generator to be used.

"They each have door shields that cover the entrances." Dengarlee informs her. "They are not very strong though. They were never meant to be used during an attack."

"We'll have to have Stephen and Demi boost the output on them." Colt suggests looking at Salis. "I think we should see if they can make them strong enough to withstand a sonic blaster cannon. It would be even better if they could rig something to cover the whole cave area even underground."

"Yes, and make sure that the doors will only allow us and the Emorphas to enter." Salis agrees. "If anyone has to fall back that far, they would have a place to go to regroup."

"Can they do all of that though? The door shields are pretty old and we've only ever used the shields for them." Belina warns them knowing that the doors had been in place for over six hundred years and only upgraded twice.

"If they're in working order, they'll find a way Belina. Both of them are good at improving electrical devices of any kind." Salis assures her with some pride. "If they can't they will make a new one."

"Why don't you go and get your people ready for the move while Salis and I go and get Demi and Stephen? We'll need someone to take them and show them where the cave is and point out the shield controls." Colt says standing. "I also want to check on how Pariben is doing. With those ships coming I want to move up our schedule a bit and see if we can't capture that patrol ship within the next twenty-four to thirty-six hours. That would be one less worry."

"I'll send Naterion to show the way. He knows the quickest route and he knows the system."

"Fine. Stephen and Demi will wait outside the ship with the air speeder. The faster they can get started the better." Salis says as they step out of the meeting house. They all agree to meet again after the evening meal to discuss their progress. Waving farewell Salis and Colt head back to the ship.

When they enter they can hear Japhet Trei over the ships intercom system shouting at either Stephen or Demi. "Stay away from me you damn machine! I told ya I don't want any of your farden food!"

"It is no longer your choice Mr. Trei. Your body is beginning to suffer because of your refusal to eat. If you will not ingest the nourishment that your body needs in the normal fashion, then I'm afraid that it will have to be forced into you." They hear Stephen speaking quietly.

There are a couple of thumps and then a groan as Stephen finally gets Trei under control. Salis and Colt enter the corridor just as Stephen walks out of the cell with Trei over his shoulder. At first Salis smiles, but then she frowns when she sees the rip in Stephen's facial covering over his left cheek, from the corner of his eye to his mouth and back towards his ear.

"What happened?"

"He attacked me with the chair. When it broke a piece caught on the side of my face and ripped the tissue."

"You had better have Demi repair it and apply an antibacterial solution. With it being living tissue it will become infected and start dying off if you don't." She tells him checking it herself and making sure that none of the upper circuits were damaged. "Once you're done with that we'll need to speak to both of you in the lounge."

"We'll be there in a couple of minutes. I want to get Trei hooked up to the feeder before his body gets any worse." He tells her and then carries Trei down to the med center.

Entering the lounge they find Pariben practicing on Trei's form. Watching him closely neither of them can detect any flaws in his appearance. When they sit down he reverts to his true form and looks at them.

"That was very good Pariben. I doubt that they will ever know that you are not the man himself." Colt tells him nodding to the chair across from them. Pariben sits down and awaits what he feels will be very important information. "We've received new information from Salis' father that we need to act upon immediately." Colt informs him just as Demi and Stephen enter the room.

Salis looks up at them. "Naterion will meet you both outside and show you to the village storage cave. I want you to see if you can modify their door shields to withstand sonic blaster cannons. They also have to be able to admit the Emorphas and our people without the shield having to be deactivated. Also if possible I want you to make it so that it shields the entire cave area above ground as well as below. You have less than three days to either modify them or replace them completely. Father will be here in four days. A little over a day later two PRC battle cruisers will arrive. We need to be ready before they get here."

"Take the air speeder. Though the cave is fairly close by, the sooner you get there, the sooner it will be done." Colt tells them wanting everything in place long before Thayer arrives.

"We'll take all the necessary tools with us for modifying or rebuilding and get started at once. In fact Demi and I have refitted the spare shield generator boosting the power output. We were planning on discussing using it as a protection for the Emorphas." Stephen tells them.

"That would be even better. Go gather what you'll need for a thorough examination. When you're ready contact the ship and have Demi's ship-self transport whatever you need directly to you including the generator. Let us know if you run into any problems."

Stephen and Demi both nod and then turn to leave. When Stephen reaches the door he turns back to Colt. "Japhet Trei is sedated while the med unit gives him the nourishment that his body needs. If you wish him out longer, just give the med unit a time period and it will administer the amount necessary." With that he continues out of the room.

Colt turns back to Pariben. "Are you ready to take on Trei's form? It might be better if you did it now and got really comfortable with it before we have you contact the patrol ship. It will let you get into character as they say."

Pariben nods and then frowns slightly. "Do you want me to take on his brain pattern as well?" Not sure if he wanted to be that much of the man for a long period of time even to act more like him.

"No, that can wait until just before you make contact with the patrol to do that." Salis tells him. "We don't know what kind of effect prolonged brain sync could have on you. Just take his physical form for now."

"While you're doing that, we'll see what we can do to help your people prepare." Colt puts in.

"When do you want to contact the patrol ship? What do you want me to say to them?" Pariben asks thinking that they should decide this beforehand.

For the next hour they go over what Pariben will say. They want to get the patrol on the planet so that they couldn't assist the PRC when they arrive. The men on the patrol ship may give them a bargaining tool to keep the PRC from attacking. When their done planning

Colt takes Pariben to the med center to touch Trei. They wanted there to be no flaws whatsoever. While Pariben is doing that Colt asks Demi's ship self for a description of Trei's physical form in minute detail.

Once Pariben has taken the other man's form, Colt has him strip so that Demi can scan him for details. When she confirms that all physical details are complete Pariben gets dressed in Trei's uniform that Stephen had removed earlier.

"Medical. Keep the patient sedated for the next forty-eight hours. Bring him to full consciousness tomorrow morning at zero-eight-thirty for no longer than twenty minutes." Colt looks over at Pariben. "That should be long enough for you to have a better grasp of his brain pattern when we contact the ship at nine."

Pariben nods his agreement and adjusts the uniform to a more comfortable position on his body. Colt watches him for several moments before leading him over to the replicator. He shows him how to use it to make up another uniform that will fit him better. "It will change the fabric if you want, but still keep the uniform design. We want you to feel as comfortable as possible while you're doing this."

"I'll try to wear this one for a while first, but thank you for showing me." Pariben leaves then to go to the room that Demi had given him earlier. He would listen to the recordings she had made of Trei's voice and practice some more.

~

The next morning Salis and Colt take Pariben back to the med center to get his brain pattern into sync with

Trei's. Once he's ready they return to the lounge where Demi has Trei's computer unit set up along with a holo image of his office.

"As far as the patrol is concerned, the transmission is still coming from Trei's former location. I will try to warn you before they do the neuro scan." Demi informs them.

"It will have to be something that won't draw suspicion." Salis warns the ship.

"I'll flash the lights twice. That shouldn't concern them and could be explained away as a power flux."

"All right Demi. Open the channel and let's get this over with." Colt says moving to the side of the computer unit with Salis so that they won't be seen.

When the captain appears Pariben goes into his act. "Captain, you can come down to the planet now. The Calidonian is distracted and I was able to disable her ships monitors." The lights flash and Pariben's eyes flick up quickly to Salis and Colt who both nod. He concentrates on the monitor.

"What was that Trei?" The captain asks frowning.

"Nothing to worry about Captain. I've been having some power fluxes the past day or two. My generator is acting up. Now back to what I was saying. If you land at the east field you'll be able to capture them. I'll send two of the changelings to lead the way."

The captain frowns then nods. "We'll be there in an hour."

"Good. You'd better bring all your men. I haven't been able to neutralize the Princess' androids and they're stronger than we thought. You can use half to distract them while the others move in for the capture."

"We'll handle it Mr. Trei. You just make sure those changelings are there to meet us when we land." The captain ends the transmission and the monitor goes blank. Before anyone can say anything Demi flashes the lights again. When Pariben starts to say something Salis holds a finger to her lips to indicate that he should remain quiet. They stand still for several minutes before Demi gives them the all clear.

"They were still monitoring through an audio feed. Probably to check if anyone else was in the room."

Pariben changes back to his normal form and sighs. "I'm glad that's over. That captain was starting to make me nervous." He shudders remembering. "If you don't need me any longer, I'll go and join the group to capture them." He raises a brow.

"That will be fine Pari. Make sure that they remember that no one is to enter the ship except Demi or Stephen. The Federation sometimes booby traps their ships in case they're boarded and the crew loses control. Stephen and Demi can deactivate any traps without setting them off when they enter." Colt reminds him before he leaves.

"I'll remind them. Will you be there?"

"Yes, but not where they can see us." Salis tells him. "Until we have control of their ship, we can't take a chance of their using it to relay our involvement before my father gets here. We'll help to capture them and subdue them, but until we know that they can't send any messages, we'll stay out of sight."

"I understand." Nodding to them Pariben quickly leaves.

Two hours later the patrol ship crew are searched and taken to one of the far buildings while Demi checks over their ship. Once all of the men are safely inside the building, Stephen activates the shield around the building to keep them inside. Two of the Emorphas bring Japhet Trei from Salis' ship to the building where the others are waiting. When Stephen nods they take Trei inside, and then quickly come out again so that the shield can be reactivated. That done Stephen turns to Salis and Colt who have just arrived to let them know what is happening so far.

"Demi has control of the ship and has wiped out all of their access programs. If any of them should escape they won't be able to use the ship against us. She's even found some subprograms with secret codes. It will take her a few hours to download everything. While she's doing that, I'm going to finish up on the cave shields. With our generator the people in the cave will be completely safe. We had to replace a lot of the circuits for the doors, but the doors themselves are of a strong alloy."

"All right Stephen. Take your time with it and add anything you feel will give the people added safety. I'll send Demi to help you as soon as she gives us her report." Salis tells him signaling that he could go now.

Stephen looks to Naterion and they head for the speeder they had left beside Naterion's home earlier.

CHAPTER 14

The Alliance ships arrive in the early hours of the morning two days later. Thayer transports down with several warrior units from each of the ships. The warriors are a mixture of most of the planets within the Alliance. They are all well trained in defense both mental and physical.

There are seven thousand men and women transported to the planet surface and placed around and inside the village. They would take the place of the Emorphas for the most part. There are still five thousand warriors on the ships to relieve any that are injured or to assist in any way needed during the fighting. The ships are moved to different positions around the planet for a better defense in space should that be necessary as well. Once in place the new cloaking devices that the Alliance science institute on Aquilia designed are activated. The cloaks cover all traces of the ships and their positions. There are no distortions of the area surrounding the ships that could give them away, so there is no indication that they are even there. They had traveled most of the distance under the cloaks, and Thayer did not believe that the PRC ships even realized that they had been right behind the Alliance ships.

Thayer sits down in the lounge and accepts the cup of parnish tea that Stephen holds out to him. "Thank you Stephen." Sipping at the hot drink he looks at Salis and Colt. "Is there a safe place for the children and others to go in case we end up having to fight? I'd rather they weren't in the villages when the PRC arrive."

"Yes there is father. Each of the villages has a storage cave within a couple of miles, but we've had all of the people come to this village. The elders meet in this village regularly, and I thought that for expediency it would be better to have everyone here in case Sarah was needed to transport everyone to the ships. Demi's already sent her the information on the cave and the areas where the people are staying. She assures me that there would be no problem transporting them from the cave if it becomes necessary." Salis assures him wanting him to know that they had considered all of the possibilities. "Stephen and Demi have even placed a ship shield generator at the cave for added protection. It will withstand sonic blaster cannons. Everyone that can't fight is already in the cave with two hundred armed Emorpha men to protect them."

"Stephen and Demi also fixed the shields so that they will admit Emorphas and members of the Alliance without having to drop the shields." Colt explains, adding that anyone injured could be taken to the cave and treated. "They have enough medical supplies to be able to deal with just about anything."

"I've made several medical units as well Your Majesty, and transported them to the cave for any serious injuries. The Emorphas won't have seen or dealt with the injuries that could occur during the fight." Demi puts in from her position behind Salis and Colt.

Thayer sees Stephen frown and wonders at its cause. Salis looks from her father to Stephen and then to Demi and nods. "That was good thinking Demi. I hadn't thought of that possibility." Salis praises her and at the same time letting her father know what had upset Stephen. "That free thinking program has really come in handy here lately father. Demi has thought of things long before either Colt or I have."

Thayer looks at his daughter for several moments before nodding his agreement. "I want to try and keep the fighting from even starting if at all possible. Where's the man responsible for this mess? I'd like to speak to him and the captain of that patrol ship and see if we can't work something out."

"His name is Japhet Trei, and he's locked up with the men from the patrol ship in one of the far buildings. We thought it best to keep them all together and away from everyone else. Neither he or the captain are willing to cooperate on any level." Colt tells him shaking his head.

"Did you tell them that the PRC ships were on their way here?" Thayer asks frowning at such actions.

"Yes, but they still said nothing. It's as if they don't believe the PRC have anything to do with them." Colt tells him with his own frown and another shake of his head.

"It's like they think that when they get here, they alone will survive the attack." Salis put in as a thought.

"They are under the assumption Thayer, that because they too work for the Federation, they will not be eliminated along with everyone else on the planet." Stephen informs him quietly.

"You say assume Stephen. Please explain your statement."

"Because they are loyal to the Federation, it is their belief that they will be released once the PRC has control. This is not the case. In both the case of Xanora and Bemissara, the Federation personnel as well as the natives were eliminated without question or exemption." Stephen explains to them.

"By the Great One Thayer!" Colt exclaims jumping up and pacing quickly around the room. "And you want to try and talk them out of this? You'll just be wasting your breath. Since they're on their way here, they've already got their orders and nothing we can say is going to change their minds."

"We don't know that for sure Colt." Salis says watching him pace. "This could be another trick to try and capture a high official of the Alliance, and who better than the man that started the Alliance?" She looks at her father.

"Is that what you believe Salis? That all of this was an elaborate trick to get officials here? To get me here?" Thayer asks looking closely at his daughter.

Salis returns her father's look. "Yes that's what I believe Father. None of this has added up from the beginning. Ships left Calidon before Colt. Some within days, some within hours. Trocon and Rachael left six hours before he did following the same route he was taking. Why wasn't their ship taken? Trocon's position is the highest after you and mother. Instead they take someone that is supposed to be known to them as only a guard." She notices that Colt has finally stopped pacing. "But somehow they knew that he was more than a guard. They knew of his connection to me and used that to draw me here and ultimately to draw you."

"But they couldn't know that I would even come Salis. I wasn't going to until Christa said that you would need me. It was all arranged for Krander to come. They couldn't know unless . . ."

"Unless someone told them." Colt finishes for him, returning to his seat beside Salis. "We've been thinking that there had to be a spy. Someone that was close to all of us and that we trusted."

"But who Colt? Who could they have . . ."

"Celeste." Salis answers as the older woman's face pops into her mind. "She came to us on Lenix Relay Station just after my seventeenth birthday. You had just finished turning down Czarina Ritduala for the second time. Remember she wanted the Alliance to loan her a couple of psi five's to probe certain members of the Federation council that she suspected of going rogue."

"That's right." Colt says looking from Salis to Thayer. "Celeste showed up two hours later saying that she was a descendant of a Manchon woman and had heard that you could arrange to send her to Manchon to look for family. Then suddenly once we left the station she asked if she could go with us instead to learn more about Manchon before going there herself."

"She offered to be one of Christa's caregivers." Salis puts in. "Mother thought it a good idea since she wasn't feeling well during her pregnancy and Celeste joined us and has been treated like a part of the family. There hasn't been too much that we've kept from her."

"But why wait so long? Why not act soon after we took her in? She's had ample opportunity with Christa. There were days when she had Christa all to herself." Thayer points out. As Salis had said they had trusted the woman and never had any guards around unless they were off Calidon.

"She was never alone with Christa father. Whenever Celeste had full care of her, Kota was always there. I don't think he's ever really liked or trusted her and she probably knows it. No, I think she was just waiting for the right time and the right vulnerability."

"And I gave her that when I could no longer stand our separation. She heard Kasmen telling me that it would be better if I was with Salis until our lifemating. My burning was getting too strong for him to help me control."

"Demi, would you please check Japhet Trei's connections again and see if he's had any contact with Czarina Ritduala. Go through his whole record and I'm sure you'll find a connection. See if he's related to Celeste as well." Salis orders.

Demi nods and leaves the room. Stephen follows her and goes to the galley to prepare Thayer and the others something to eat. He was sure that Thayer hadn't eaten for a while and Salis and Colt hadn't eaten much at the evening meal the night before.

"I'll contact your mother and have her place Celeste into custody until we return."

"Christa is already doing that father." Salis says with a slight smile. "When Celeste's image popped into my mind, I automatically sent to Christa. She's gone straight to mother with my thoughts."

Thayer nods and stretches a little to relieve some of the tension in his shoulders. "When is first light?"

Colt looks at the chronometer. "In about two hours."

"Well then, as soon as I get something to eat and a fresh change of clothes, I suggest we get ready for those cruisers." He says standing just as Stephen walks into the room with a laden tray of food and drink.

~

By the time the PRC cruisers arrive, everyone is in place. The women, children, elderly, and infirm are safely in the cave protected by their men and an extra hundred from the Alliance. The children understand that they could not leave the caves until their parents tell them that it's safe. They don't really mind being stuck in the cave though, because now they can explore as they have never been allowed to do before.

Pariben once again takes Japhet Trei's form and is prompted by Thayer to try and convince the commanders of both ships to leave. "They've figured out everything Commander Olivinite and intend to go to the other planet leaders unless you back off. They've already sent out messages to other Alliance members."

"How could they have learned of your mission Trei, unless you told them?"

"I have only told them what I was told they could know Commander. The rest they figured out on their own."

"Where are their ships that arrived before us Mr. Trei? Our scanners showed six battle cruisers capable of carrying up to four thousand men each. They were stationary above the planet for nearly two hours and then just disappeared."

"I know nothing of any other ships commander except for the Princess' ship that is here on the planet."

"What of the patrol ship sent to act as reinforcement? Why is it now on the planet and not out here where it should be?"

"They came down as a security measure when I informed the captain of the situation. Commander, again I must ask you to leave. Your presence here is jeopardizing all that we are trying to avoid and will not help us to get what we want."

Another image appears next to the commander and whispers in his ear. Commander Olivinite frowns and looks up at the image of Japhet Trei. He nods to the other officer before speaking to Trei. "Japhet Trei, you are here by declared a traitor to the Federation and to your mistress. You are to surrender yourself at once or suffer the consequences of your actions along with everyone else on the planet."

Thayer has Pariben move away from the monitor and takes his place. "Commander Olivinite, you know who I am?" He waits for the other man's acknowledgment. "Then you know that if you attack this planet you will be in violation of the Federation's primary law against attacking neutral leaders. Since the Emorphas of Brightstar have asked formally for and received the protection of the Telepathic Alliance of Planets, the Federation and any of its members no longer has any jurisdiction over this world. I suggest that you and the other commander turn your ships around and leave. There will be no eradication done on this world to these people. They have done nothing to warrant your presence here." He says calmly hoping that the man will listen. "We are willing and able to defend this planet and its people if need be. They will not be used by your mistress or anyone else to defraud or control anyone. The Alliance will make sure that the rest of the Federation leaders know of what she has been up to no matter what happens here today."

Already under orders from Czarina Ritduala to gain control of the Emorphas at any cost, Commander Olivinite orders the attack without flinching. Thayer nods grimly and ends the communication.

'Everyone prepare for an attack, they're on their way down. Remember, no lives are to be taken unless there is no other way. We are not killers and murderers. All weapons on deep stun only. All ships are to disable their ships without loss of life.'

CHAPTER 15

Though Thayer would like nothing better than to order Salis to stay on her ship, he knows that they will need her abilities. He also knows that she would not follow such an order. She would take it as an insult and a question towards her capability to use her abilities in an extremely dangerous situation.

When the Alliance team disables several hundred of the Federation's people, the fighting escalates and the ships soon join in. After three hours of fighting, Demi warns of the approach and arrival of several more Federation ships. Within six hours the Alliance is out numbered two to one, but they continue to hold their own.

The Alliance ships are able to disable the two PRC's and one of the new cruisers. These three have power loss to their engines and weapons, but are otherwise unharmed. The Alliance ships have sustained little or no damage by using their cloaks to cover their whereabouts before each attack. The fighting continues into the next day and begins getting more deadly. Where the day before most injuries were minor, today they are becoming more serious and life threatening. During the worst of this Salis is contacted by Christa.

'I don't . . . have . . . . time . . . to talk . . . to you . . . right now Christa.'

'Don't talk Lissa, just listen. You have to release your inner fire now. There will be many unnecessary deaths if you don't. Only your Firepetal and Daddy's Starhawk can stop the fighting before it's too late. There isn't much time left Lissa. Our people are suffering more than they have to. Use your inner fire Lissa, it's the only way to stop all of this and save lives.'

Christa breaks off their contact and Salis lets what she said slip from her mind as she draws some Federation men away from the cave. She watches as Colt and some of the Aquilians fly into the air and open fire upon the men that have several Emorphas caught in a crossfire. She puts off talking to her father for almost two hours. Towards the end of the second hour Salis feels a burning pain in her chest and head. Knowing that she wasn't hit by anything, she looks around for Colt and sees him falling to the ground. Two Aquilians catch him before he hits and carry him to her ship. Knowing that she can no longer put it off, she approaches her father and tells him of what Christa had told her.

"I put it off when I should have come to you right away. Now Colt's been hurt and I could have prevented it from happening."

"You don't know that for sure sweetheart. It could have happened anyway. Besides, both you and Colt knew of the dangers, especially Colt." Thayer isn't sure how much power Salis has, but he agrees with Christa that their other selves are the only option they have left. Too many of their people had been injured and several had been killed, possibly even Colt. They had to do something and quickly.

"Okay we're going to do it Salis, but you have to be prepared for the power that you'll have. It will be at least ten times stronger than your normal abilities." He warns her and then calls his personal guard over to create a shield around them until they begin to change. Once they're in place, he explains to Salis how to call up her inner fire. "Imagine a small flame deep within your heart of hearts. Picture it growing with every beat of your heart. As it grows it consumes you, becoming more a part of you until you are the flame. Embrace it and accept it as a part of you."

Salis follows his instructions and soon feels the power of the fire flowing through and around her. When Thayer notices the change in her aura he begins his own transformation. Within minutes their transformation is complete and they begin to stop the fighting. Slowly and carefully they render the Federation people unconscious and then send them back to their ships. They send them back in groups of five hundred until there are none left on the planet. Starhawk must remind Firepetal several times not to take any lives. He knows that she has felt the satisfaction that several of the men felt for the injuries and deaths they have caused during this fight.

'We can do them no more harm Firepetal. We have what is needed to be sure that this doesn't happen again. All we have to do is send them back. No one else needs to die.'

Once all of the Federation men are back on their ship, Starhawk touches all of their minds. He tells them that the Alliance will not tolerate such actions again by any member of the Federation. *'We will not wait as long as we did here, to do what must be done. When we bring action against your mistress you will all testify against her and tell the truth. None of you will be held responsible unless you were one of her advisors and totally agreed with her actions. You will admit it if you were. You will remember none of this until the proper time and place. What you will remember is that we defeated you and how we defeated you. You will remember that we never give up.'*

Firepetal permanently disables their weapons and communications, she also temporarily disables their engines. They would be able to start them again when it was necessary. When she's done Starhawk moves closer to her until their fires begin to mingle. Concentrating, they combine their powers and send all of the Federation ships back towards their origin. When they are within their sector they will be able to restart their engines and continue on.

Before changing back to their human forms, they repair their own ships, making sure that everything is once more in good working order. When they finally do return to their human forms, Salis rushes back to her ship to be at Colt's side. Several of the Emorphas, including Belina and the other leaders are standing outside the ship. None try to stop her as she rushes past them, understanding why she doesn't stop to speak with them.

Running to their cabin, Salis comes to a halt just inside the door and looks at Colt laying so still on their bed. She looks at Demi who is standing at the foot of the bed hoping that she will tell her that he will be all right.

Demi looks back at her and slowly shakes her head. "I'm sorry Salis. The med unit did all that it could. There's just too much damage for it to completely heal him. Our healers can't do anything either. It's beyond their capabilities."

Biting her lower lip against a building scream, Salis nods and walks slowly over to the bed. Kneeling down beside it she gently takes Colt's hand in her own. At her touch his eyes open and he smiles slightly at her. Not able to speak aloud he links their minds.

'We did it atma. We saved the Emorpha from certain death. Now they'll be safe and able to do what they enjoy without fear of someone using them.'

'Yes my love. We helped them all.' Tears start to fall down her cheeks.

'Don't cry love. If I am to die at least I will do it with honor and with the knowledge that it wasn't for nothing.'

'I don't want you to die Colt. We've only just come back together. We still have to be lifemated. Please don't leave me. We'll find a way to heal you. Maybe grandmother Royanna or Cassie can heal you.'

'You know I don't want to go Salis, and we would never get to Manchon in time. The Great One calls me to him. Even though we've never gone through all the ceremonies, to me, in my heart of hearts, we are already lifemates. We have been since we first met. I will always be with you, always be a part of you as you will with me. Through all eternity Salis. I claim you as my own. I love you Salis Starhawk Blackwood. Now until forever.'

'As I claim you as my own and love you Colton Blackwood. Now until forever.'

Colt's eyes close and his breathing begins to slow. Carefully Salis lays his hand down and turns to

Demi. "Couldn't we put him into suspension and take him . . . ?"

Demi shakes her head. "No Salis. He would never survive the process, and even if he did, I know that he would not survive being brought out of it. His functions are all too weak and the shock of reanimation would kill him for sure."

Salis looks back at Colt's still body noticing that his breathing is becoming more labored and is almost nonexistent. Looking at him she thinks to herself that there has to be some way to save him. The Great One wouldn't just take him like this. Rachael had once told them that they would have many children, and they would bring new hope to men for a long time to come.

It's not his time to go. What must I do to save him? It must be something that I have to do, otherwise the med unit would have been able to heal him, or even the healers. Wondering what she can do she closes her eyes. Suddenly images begin forming in her mind. They are images of when she was a young girl and she and her parents were on Earth. Brockton had been poisoned and no one could do anything to save him. A voice had spoken to her and told her that her touch could heal. Her touch could stop a wrongful death and add new life. She had the healing fire within her. The fire that burns brightly but never burns, never harms or kills. She had to call on the fire and believe in it. All wounds, all sickness would be healed. Those whom she healed would be given the chances that would otherwise have been taken from them. Trusting that voice, Salis had put her hands on Brockton and called to that fire. She asked that the poison be burned from his body and that his damaged tissues be healed and made whole once more.

It had been done and Brockton had recovered with no ill effects. His healing had also repaired the damage that had prevented him from fathering children.

Salis opens her eyes and looks at Colt again. She wonders if the fire she remembers is the same fire that made her the Firepetal. Once again she hears that voice telling her to trust in her fire. She is now one with the fire and it will not harm as long as she believes in it and in herself. *'You can do all things through Him that strengthens you.'* Nodding to the voice she hears, she smiles and stands up.

Thayer stops to talk to the Emorphas before entering the ship. He wants to give Salis time alone with Colt knowing that it would be the only time she had. One of the Alliance healers had informed him of Colt's condition as soon as it was known. He has had to fight his own anger and his urge to avenge the meaningless assault on the young man.

"I want to take Japhet Trei and the patrol ship crew back with us. With their testimony and the records they've kept, we'll make sure that nothing like this ever happens again." He says speaking to Belina and Keley.

"I'm afraid that won't be possible your Majesty. The building that they were being held in was completely destroyed just after the fighting began. None survived." Keley informs him sadly. They had never planned to harm any of those people.

"One man did live long enough to ask our forgiveness. He also said that he never thought that it would go this far." Belina adds shaking her head over the senselessness. "It was senseless to kill those men. They never had the chance to explain what had happened to them. To defend themselves at all."

"Some of the Federation leaders do a lot of senseless things Mistress Belina. That's one of the reasons why the Alliance was set up. To make sure that such senseless acts don't occur if we can help it." Thayer tells her sadly. "Sometimes we don't learn of things until it's too late to do anything about them or to gather proof that something is wrong. With luck we will soon restore peace and unity to all the worlds and such things as happened here will never happen again."

"May the Great One bless us with that day in our lifetimes." Keley says softly, and the others nod their agreement.

"If you will excuse me. I need to go to my daughter to be with her at this time."

Belina and Keley nod their understanding and watch him enter the ship. Both know that their new friends will be suffering greatly with this loss. When they kneel to pray for the young man that had saved their people, those around them do the same hoping that it will be enough.

Thayer walks to the cabin that Salis and Colt share and takes a deep breath before entering. As he steps into the room he sees Salis turn into Firepetal once again. When he recovers from the shock of her quick change, he sees her reaching for Colt's body. Before he can stop her, since none of them knew what could happen to someone without the inner fire, her fiery arms wrap around Colt and easily lift him up.

As she takes him into her arms, Firepetal calls out to the Great One. *'Oh Great giver of life, hear my call to spare this man taken before his time. Give unto him the fire within me. He is more worthy of this gift then I will ever be. He will know better how to use it. He is my other half, he makes me whole and complete. Without him I would be lost and a drift in a life with no joy, no love, no warmth. Though I have a small part of him within me, it would fade with time and one day be lost. If a life is needed, take mine instead. Give unto him my fire, and he will always have a part of me with him. A part of me that will not fade with time, will not one day be lost. I ask this not for myself, but for him and our people. Let him live out his life to the fullest and never will I regret giving my life for his. I know that he would do the same for me, for our love of each other is that strong.'*

Several fiery tears fall onto Colt's forehead and chest, and within moments the fire of those tears go around his body and he begins to glow with their light. Thayer stands there watching as the tears of fire fall but do not burn. He watches them spread over Colt's body and then watches as they enter his body and fill him with an inner glow. As he watches the wounds he had received begin to heal and within minutes are completely gone and there is no sign that they had ever been.

Firepetal gently lowers the still glowing body back onto the bed and gently kisses his cheek. She straightens up and sighs. Salis returns to her physical form and collapses. Thayer moves quickly to catch her and then lays her on the bed beside Colt. Stepping back he signals for Demi to check them both out.

Demi runs her hand first over Salis and then over Colt. "Salis has slipped into a coma Thayer. Colt is doing fine. All of his injuries are healed and there are no indications that he was ever injured internally or externally."

"Why has Salis gone into a coma? She wasn't even scratched during the fighting." Thayer frowns not understanding why she would go into a coma.

"It could be her body's response to everything that's happened over the past forty-eight hours Thayer. She's never had to deal with this level of destruction before, this level of violence. That something happened to Colt and he almost died, was just too much for her to deal with on a conscious level."

"How long will this last?" Thayer asks touching Salis' leg and not getting any response at all. He tries to touch her mind but can feel nothing.

"Until her mind has accepted all that she's seen and done she'll be like this. I could bring her out of it, but we would risk doing irreparable damage to her psyche. She has to come out of this on her own."

"All right Demi, if you're sure. Please continue to monitor her condition and let me know the minute there's any change. Especially if . . . if she gets worse. I need to contact her mother and let her know that everything is under control here." He looks again at Salis and Colt before leaving the room.

Going to the lounge he walks in on the others waiting for him. He tells them that young Colt would recover with no indication that he was ever injured. He explains that Salis' fire had healed him and that they were both resting. "Go and tell the others and start accessing the damage to the villages and land. Though we tried to keep the fighting here it spread to the other villages. If possible I want us to repair the destruction. What can't be repaired we will replace. Two of the Emorphas leaders are out front, have them send people with you to help in the assessment. That's all for now." They all nod and leave him alone in the lounge.

Stretching out on the sofa, Thayer closes his eyes and reaches out to Leyla. *'We've done it Love. The Emorphas are now completely free of the Federation. I've made them members of the Alliance to insure that there won't be any problems. Start the paperwork will you?'*

'How bad were the losses?'

'A lot less than I thought there would be. We may have lost about a thousand, or a little more but not much more than that. There were a dozen battle cruisers by the time we ended the fighting. You can tell Christa that Salis did fine. She's fully accepted her fire and it runs strongly through her.'

'She'll be glad to hear that. How are Salis and Colt? They weren't hurt were they? Christa is being very agitated.'

'They're both fine. Colt was injured but he's as good as new. They're both sleeping right now, regaining the strength they used during the fight.'

'Was there much damage done to the Emorphas homes?'

'I have people out accessing the damage now. We'll try to repair what we can and replace what we can't. Japhet Trei and the patrol crew were executed during the fight. The building they were locked in was completely destroyed. I should have had them moved to one of the ships before the fighting started.'

'You couldn't have known that it would happen Thayer. Who could? It's not human to kill your own people during a war.'

'Yes, but we knew that the PRC had the tendency of killing all present, no matter if they were loyal or not. Now we know that they will in any situation.'

'Do we have enough to approach the Federation's High Council?'

'More than enough. Demi and Stephen have recorded everything from start to finish. We'll also have the testimony of the entire fleet that was here when we need it. Even if Czarina and her followers attempted to get rid of those that fought here, they'd have a problem explaining the deaths of close to sixty thousand men and women. I made sure that they would all be willing to testify truthfully when the time comes. What about Celeste? Has she said anything to explain her part in all of this?'

'Yes she has. She said that she had no choice. Apparently Czarina has been holding her young daughter until she's satisfied that things are going the way she planned. Czarina promised Celeste that she would release the girl and send her to her when everything was done.'

'Instead she'll probably kill the girl and send someone to kill Celeste as well so there is no one to link them together.'

'I thought of that too, that's why I had one of my father's people go in and get the child. She's on her way here. When Celeste told me everything I got the image of her daughter and sent it to father. As soon as his man got to the girl we ported her and the agent to one of our ships that was in the area. Brockton and Selina helped me with the porting, and I'm sure that Christa was in on it to. They should arrive here in a week.'

'Good. Put Krander and his men on guard duty around her. Have him take her to Kaden until we need her. We can send her daughter to her after she arrives. No one but our closest advisors is to know any of this.'

'Agreed love. How long before you return home?'

'I'm not sure. I want to be sure that everything is going good before we leave here. I'll let you know when we plan to leave. Kiss the children for us and give them our love.'

'I will. Take care my love, tell Salis I'm very proud of her, and to get in touch with her sister as soon as she can. I don't think Christa will settle until she hears from her herself.'

After agreeing, Thayer ends their link and just lays there for several minutes. He thinks to himself that he should have told her everything. When she found out that he didn't tell her everything, he was the one that was going to need healing. Even knowing that, he just couldn't tell her and have her worrying needlessly. Both Salis and Colt would be fine and there was nothing that his mate could do even if she were here. Salis' mind was completely shut off to them until she was ready to open up again and deal with everything that had happened. Finally he sits up and looks around. He really should get himself something to eat. He couldn't remember when the last time was that he ate anything solid. All he could remember was someone handing him energy drinks every few hours.

Before he can stand, the door to the lounge opens and Stephen enters with a tray full of food. "I figured that you would be ready for a meal to fill you now that the last of the energy drinks has left your system. It has been nearly three days since you've eaten and the energy drinks don't really have all that your body needs to stay healthy."

"Thank you Stephen. I was just going to go and fix myself something." Thayer admits as the android sets the tray down in front of him. He nods for Stephen to sit as he starts eating. After slacking off the worst of his hunger he begins questioning Stephen. "How many of the Emorphas did we lose during the fighting?"

"Two hundred and seventy-eight. Close to four hundred were injured but will recover."

"How many of our own were lost?"

"One thousand one hundred and seventeen. Most were killed when the ships opened fire. All of the injured are being treated by the med units and healers that have come down from the ships."

"What about the damage done to the villages? How bad is it?"

"Several of the homes and businesses were destroyed completely in most of the villages. Some sustained minor structural damage. I'm still waiting on the reports about the farms surrounding the villages. I believe that they will not have sustained much if any damage. They would have been considered more valuable to the PRC then the villages themselves."

Thayer finishes his meal and sits back drinking his coffee. "What about the patrol ship? Did it survive or was it destroyed as well?"

"They attempted to destroy it, but Demi had modified the shield output to protect it. Though she had already downloaded their main computer system, she hadn't gotten to a lot of the personal logs. She'll finish downloading those as soon as Salis wakes. Until then, she'll stay at Salis' side unless you order her to do otherwise."

Thinking that it was exactly what Stephen wanted him to do, Thayer shakes his head. "No, there's nothing she needs to deal with in her body. Her ship self can handle any questions we have. I'd rather keep her monitoring Salis' condition until she comes out of this coma."

"Very well. If you no longer need me, I'll go and do a check on the med units she placed in the cave." He stands and waits for any further instructions.

"That will be fine Stephen. If you need anything have Sarah transport it down to you." Stephen nods and leaves the room. Thayer shakes his head at the androids reaction. If he didn't know better he would swear that Stephen was becoming more and more human every year. When they got back to Calidon he was going to have the people at the science institute run a full diagnostic on both him and Sarah. Something was definitely going on with those two computer units that wasn't normal.

"Thayer, Colt has awakened and my mobile unit would like you to come to the room."

"I'll be there as soon as I clean up Demi."

CHAPTER 16

"It was very strange Demi. Like I was floating away with no sense of myself. Then suddenly I was surrounded by this beautiful fire and I knew that it was Salis and that I couldn't leave her, not yet." Colt explains sitting on the side of the bed holding Salis' hand.

"She wouldn't let you go." Demi informs him quietly. "She wouldn't believe that there was no way to bring you back. When she transformed I knew what she was going to do. Then her tears fell on you, I knew that it would work. Your body absorbed the fire of her tears and they became a part of you."

Colt nods and looks back at Salis. "Why doesn't she wake up though? I'm fine now and the Emorphas are safe. There's no reason for her to remain like this."

"I'm afraid that she's slipped into an even deeper coma since you woke Colt." Demi explains just as Thayer enters the room.

"What do you mean that she's in a deeper coma?" Thayer demands stopping beside the bed and frowning at Demi.

Demi looks from Salis to Thayer and back again. "When Colt woke, she went into a deeper coma. The light coma she was in at first held only until Colt was completely healed and he no longer needed her support to keep him going."

"Then bring her out of it. This has gone on long enough." Thayer demands glaring at Demi.

"As I told you before Majesty, we can't bring her out of the coma without seriously damaging her psyche. She has to bring herself out. It isn't a normal coma for me to interfere with." She explains carefully. "Even if I wanted to, and you ordered it as you just did, I would still have to tell you no. I can't go against the programming she gave before she healed Colt, even with the free thinking program. She knew that something like this would happen and wanted no intervention. Should I attempt to go against my programming, I will automatically stop functioning. Both this form and my ship self will be no more."

Thayer closes his eyes knowing that he would not officially order Demi to go against her programming. She was very important to Salis and he didn't want to destroy her just because he was impatient to have Salis awake and whole again. "It's all right Demi. I understand. I just wish that there was some way to reach her. I've tried several times, but her mind is completely cut off from me. She's even cut herself off from Christa."

Colt frowns at this. He had never known a time when Salis cut herself off from her baby sister deliberately except when they were having sex. He closes his eyes to reach out to her. *'Salis, it's time to wake up now. I'm fine and waiting for you. Come back to me atma. We're meant to be together you know that. If you don't come back then I will lay down beside you and join you wherever you are, where ever you go. I would give my life for you Salis, you know this. Don't leave me.'*

For several minutes there is no response, though he continues to call to her. He tells her that she is upsetting Christa and that she needs her big sister. When he finally feels her mind stirring, he calls even more. He tells her of his love and all that they would do when they were finally lifemated. After several more minutes Salis begins to move and her eyes open. They look at each other and Colt takes her into his arms and lets her cry out all her grief and anguish over what has happened and what she was forced to do. When she finally stops she looks up at Thayer and then over to Demi and back again when Demi nods to her.

"Thank you." She whispers to her father.

"You're welcome little one. I couldn't hurt her knowing that in the end I would be hurting you as well." Thayer smiles down at her. "We'll leave you two to yourselves for a while. I have some things that I need to discuss with Demi. When you're able, you need to contact your sister and calm her. When you went into your coma she became very agitated." Salis nods. Thayer nods to Demi and together they leave the room closing and locking the door behind them.

After coming out of her self-induced coma, Salis is still feeling drained and remains in bed for several days. Shortly after she had awaked and her father had left she had tried to contact Christa but was too weak. Christa had felt her and reached out to her, they had both cried and Salis assured her that she was all right and would contact her when she was feeling stronger. Colt hardly ever leaves her side except when he is needed to help with the reconstruction of the Emorphas villages.

The buildings that were totally destroyed are replaced with specially designed new ones brought by an Aquilian freighter. The damage to the planet is harder to repair. There are several deep holes that were created when the ships had opened fire upon the planet. Different surface layers were fused together by the intense heat generated by the blasts. For these it is decided to make them into reservoirs for extra power. However, the Emorphas have many advanced tools and equipment, their technical knowledge has almost completely vanished. They retain only enough to keep their two ships running and the door shields at the caves going at minimum.

The Alliance would bring them up to date without interfering too much with their natural way of life. As new things are brought down, their function and how to work on them is taught to selected Emorphas who would take over the care and maintenance of the pieces. This is the main time when Colt is needed. He uses his knowledge of the Emorphas minds to implant the information that they will need. When Salis is fully recovered she helps to implant the information as well.

Two weeks after defeating the Federation, Thayer suggests that they return home. It is agreed that they will leave two of their ships to help finish and to act as planetary guards. Until matters are settled with the Federation this would insure that nothing happened to any of the people.

Before they leave Thayer meets with the elders. "You have already been registered as a planet under our protection, and the ships are meant to warn off any attempts at retaliation." Thayer explains to Belina, Keley, and Dengarlee. "Whether you join or not, we will always protect you."

"We thank you for that and for risking your people to help us." Belina says bowing her head as she remembers all of the Alliance people that had died to save their people. "If not for you we would still be under the Federations control."

"No thanks are necessary Mistress Belina. We would have helped anyone in your situation as any sentient being should do." He assures her. "We would like one of you to return to Calidon with us to talk with our High Council. Pariben too would need to go, to add what his mind picked up from Japhet Trei."

"How could you do that?" Dengarlee asks frowning. "Pariben is himself with none of Trei within him."

"That is essentially true Den, but his subconscious mind holds a part of Japhet Trei that we did not expect." Salis tells him gently. "When he took on Trei's form the last time he had no physical contact. He took his form without any problems. He also took on his brain pattern. We believe that a part of Pari's mind took and stored away parts of Trei's memories. If he did we can remove those memories and enhance them to computer images. Then we would erase that information from his mind and leave nothing of Trei but Pari's own memories of him. It is completely safe and will not harm Pari in any way." She assures him knowing that he was worried about the younger man's mind.

Dengarlee stares at her for several moments before nodding his agreement. Thayer also nods at Salis' ability to explain well.

"Which of you will travel with Pariben back to Calidon? It shouldn't take too long to take your statements and have a judgment made." Thayer looks at each of them as they look at each other. It was then that he realizes that they do have some type of telepathic ability. He blinks when they look back at him.

"I will go with you to your home." Belina informs them. "Keley and Dengarlee have no wish to leave our home at this time. They will stay and continue to help our people come to terms with what has happened. Maybe later when things are more settled for our people they will travel to the other worlds."

"That will be fine. Would you like someone to go with you?" Colt asks her wanting her to feel comfortable.

"If you wouldn't mind, I would like to take my daughter Shayara with me. She would enjoy it, and I think she needs to get away from here for a little while."

"She will be welcome Belina." Salis assures her. She had gotten to know Shayara while they were there and would welcome her company. "If she likes, she could stay with us for a while when you return home. I know that this hasn't been easy for her or any of the other troupe members. They still blame themselves for what happened to your people, though the fault is not theirs."

"We'll see. The final decision will be hers of course." Belina looks at Thayer. "When will we be leaving?"

"In two days. We'll take Salis' ship and the others will follow. We'll get there in about a week at top speed."

"That will be fine. That will give Den, Keley and I time to talk things over with our people and have a full decision for you on whether or not we will join your Alliance." She tells him looking at the others. "Though I imagine that all of our people will agree to join."

The meeting breaks up and everyone goes to finish other work and to prepare for the departure in two days. Thayer wants to be sure that everything is well under control before they leave and to know of anything else the Emorphas may need that can be sent to them.

During the week that it takes them to get to Calidon Salis, Colt, and Thayer tell the Emorphas about Calidon and the Telepathic Alliance of Planets. Demi shows them holograms of each member world and gives them the history of each world and its people.

Belina, Shayara, and Pariben ask question about how each planet came to join the Alliance and what they contributed. They ask about the social structures, the arts and sciences, and the moral standards that each has lived by. Though most of their questions can be easily answered, there are some that they are told must be put to the people of those worlds.

"A lot of what we learn is learned while our people stay on the different worlds." Salis tells them. "The best way to learn about another culture is to live in that culture and see for yourself what it is like to be of it. I think that is really what the Alliance is all about. Learning about and accepting others. When you can accept the differences in others, you can better understand and accept differences in yourself."

"Has there ever been any that it was hard to accept?" Shayara asks not believing that everything on any world was completely acceptable.

Salis frowns considering the question. "Yes, there are some instances where things are hard to accept. The Taquiery are people that eat raw meat, but they understand that most others do not do so. When they are with others not of their people they will eat their meat lightly cooked so that it is more acceptable, but no one forces them to do so, and they do not insist that others eat as they do when on their world."

Both Shayara and Belina shudder at the thought of placing bloody meat into their mouths. Neither of them planned on ever visiting that world themselves, but maybe some of the others would. They would definitely need to get more information about the other member worlds and try to prepare themselves for anything that even remotely sounded strange to them. They did not want to offend anyone by being revolted or making a comment about something that is a natural part of another's life.

When they finally reach Calidon, all of the Alliance High Council are present, as are all of Colt's family. While Thayer introduces Belina and the others, Colt and Salis are checked over by the Blackwoods to assure themselves that both are fine. Christa has not left her sister's side since she stepped off the ship.

"Merri contacted us when she felt you struck Colt." Cassandra Knightrunner says looking over her baby brother once more. "We all felt it, but Merri knew that you were hurt badly. Are you sure that you're all right?"

"I'm fine Cassie. Salis was able to heal me before it was too late." He smiles at Salis standing near his twin Merri. Salis smiles back at him, but her smile is not as bright as it normally would have been. While the others talk to Colt, Merri has a silent conversation with Salis.

'What's wrong Lissa? You're still upset.'

'It was my fault that Colt got hurt as bad as he did Merri. If I hadn't waited so long to talk to father and to transform, he wouldn't have nearly died. A lot of people wouldn't have died if I hadn't been afraid of that part of myself.'

'You can't go on blaming yourself for that Salis. There is no guaranty that Colt wouldn't have been just as badly hurt sooner or that those warriors wouldn't have died anyway. All happenings have a purpose and all purposes have a reason. We may not understand or like them, but we must live with them. It's possible that those things had to happen for you to transform.'

'But it was all so senseless Merri. All those people died for . . . '

'Don't you dare say that they died for no reason Salis Starhawk. The Great One has a reason for all things and you know that. It's not for us to understand or question Him, but to accept both the good and the bad. He will never forsake us. He will guide us and help us through all of our trials. Even this one.'

Salis looks at her and knows that she's right. "Yes, you're right Merri. He did show me how to heal Colt when there was no other way. I still plan to pay my debt to the families of those that lost someone at Brightstar. It will help me to know that I have thanked them in some small way for their sacrifice."

"Do what you must Lissa, but don't blame yourself. None of those who died would, and neither will their families. All of us knew that there was a chance that some wouldn't be coming home, and we knew that it was their choice to go and fight." Merri says giving her arm a tight squeeze and then gives her a hug. Everyone that had gone with Thayer had made the choice of their own free will and they all realized that it was the right thing to do.

"Hey you two! Come on, we're going to the Conference Center." Colt calls to them and then walks over and steps between them. He looks down at Salis. "Are you all right atma?"

"I'm fine Colt. Everything's going to be fine now." She assures him looking past him to Merri. "Everything is just fine now."

Colt looks from one to the other and frowns slightly. He had seen them linking and had tried to listen in, but Merri had blocked him out and told him to give them some space. He knew that Salis had still been bothered by what had happened on Brightstar, but whatever his twin had said to her must have settled her mind. He could now feel the return of Salis' old aura patterns returning strong and it was now clear of the darkness that it had when she had awakened from her coma. Somehow his twin had found a way to heal his lifemate and he would never forget it. One day he would repay her for that gift.

"All right, we know that Czarina Ritduala and her group are behind what took place on the Emorphas home world, Brightstar. By themselves they're no problem, but together they make up almost a fourth of the Federation High Council." Baylynx Rahl, the High King of Panthera states. "How do we get all of the others on the council to listen to our charges against her and the others?"

Murmurs can be heard all through the conference hall at his question. It was a question on all of their minds. Thayer stands and holds up his hands for silence. Once the room quiets down again he answers the question himself.

"We use one of her own men to get their attention. Japhet Trei was well known to all of the High Council through the work that he did for them. The Council all know who he took his orders from. Pariben Ternasher's mind absorbed most of Japhet Trei's memories when they had mental contact. Pariben is the Emorpha that helped Salis and Colt to capture the Federation patrol ship. When we landed, Stephen and Demi took him to the institute to have those memories removed and placed onto a memory crystal. They will be enhanced and restored, then cataloged for the express purpose of showing to the other members of the Federation Council. There is no doubt that some of those memories will be of plots against the other members of the council. If we can locate all of those memories and isolate them, we can save them to separate crystals and send copies to the members that are affected. They will listen to what we have to say. They will want to stop them just as much as we do."

The others nod that this would definitely get the attention of the High Council. A Savônian stands to question something.

"King Thayer. I am Creigh from Savôn."

"Yes Creigh, what do you wish to know?"

"Why don't you just have this Trei fellow testify himself? Won't the Federation council question a memory crystal against their own people that comes from us?" He asks before sitting back down.

"At first they might, but after they run a scan on it they will accept it. All telepaths that work for the Federation have had a neurological scan and their patterns on all levels recorded. Any deviation of those patterns would be noted immediately. With what Pariben did, his abilities allowed him to pick up those patterns completely. Only we know that it was reproduced and that the crystals are not being made from the man himself." Creigh nods his understanding of this as do several others. "As for your first question on why we don't have Japhet Trei testify, it is because he can't. He was life-ended on Brightstar during the fight."

Thayer looks out at the people and sees their shock at this news. "We did not take his life or the lives of those that were being held with him. They died when the people that they worked with, and whom they trusted, destroyed the building where they were being held. If he were still alive we would convince him to testify for himself."

Next a Pantherian stands and is told that she can speak. "I am Sonda Javon of Panthera."

Baylynx stands to address her. "Yes Sonda, what is it that you wish to know?"

"When we get them to listen, what will we ask for? Will they give the Emorphas compensation for the destruction done to their world, to their people? And what of our own people that lost their lives defending them?"

Baylynx looks at Thayer before answering her question and receives a nod to speak freely. "We will ask for the removal of Czarina Ritduala and her four coconspirators from all Federation councils, and that they be replaced with members chosen by the non-allied worlds to insure that people of the same mind are not put into power again. For the Emorphas we will ask for technology that will make their lives easier without taking away their uniqueness or their way of life. We will also ask that they be paid in full for the performances that they were unable to do because of their enforced captivity on their world. The revenue that their performing troupe brought in purchased things that their people used and needed. For our people and the Emorphas that died, we will ask for compensation as well in the form of credits that would be paid to any warriors family should they die in battle. For Princess Salis and Lord Colton, we will ask compensation for their pain and suffering of both the physical and mental. We will also insist that they replace Lord Colton's ship as well as the valuables that were lost when the ship was destroyed." He finishes and sits down with a nod to Faucon of Aquilia, who stands and finishes.

"We will also insist that all Federation ships entering space that is occupied by an Alliance world must first have Alliance Council's permission before doing so. Any violators will be charged a thousand credits for every person aboard the ship. Those credits will be used by the Alliance as a whole. It will also be let known that the Telepathic Alliance of Planets will no longer stand by and let others suffer needlessly for the greed of others. Whether they are part of the Alliance or not. We will use any means necessary to bring such people to justice. If the Federation will not deal with them, then we will. However, no one, no one will ever be put to death without just cause. We will not go out and kill anyone for whatever reason. Only those that are of total blackness, totally evil and cannot or will not change, will be life-ended by our people. This will also apply to our own people as well."

With Faucon's last statement gasps can be heard throughout the hall. Faucon sits down and Thayer stands back up holding up his hands for silence once again. They knew that this would cause upset, but it had to be said and they would follow through with it.

"You all know what happened here before Leyla and I became the rulers of Calidon. The man that we life-ended cared nothing for his people or anyone else. A person such as that is a danger to all who come into contact with them. If given the chance they would take the life of a child to save their own. Such a person is not and never will be seen as a necessary part of our society. If you believe otherwise think of that child as your own. Would you let such a person kill your child to save his or her own life? Would you take a child's live to save your own?" He looks around at those gathered. "Would you take any innocent life to save your own? Think long and hard about this people. No life will be taken unless there is no way to redeem that soul from darkness. However, if needed we will do so. This meeting is adjourned."

The High Council stands and leaves the hall knowing that most of the people would think about the last part of the meeting for a long time to come. Some would never accept it, but they also would not interfere if it should ever come to pass that such an evil person was to touch upon their lives in any way. No matter what the Federation did, the Telepathic Alliance would see to it that people no longer lived in fear.

~

Rachael and Royanna closely examine Belina, Shayara, and Pariben, testing their mental abilities very carefully. They all have the ability to take on another's brain patterns and store them in their subconscious mind. Their minds also have the ability to send and receive telepathic messages amongst their own people, but it is more difficult for them to send or receive from others. After several tests, both Rachael and Royanna agree that in time the Emorphas will be able to communicate telepathically with the other members of the Alliance.

"You already have the ability to communicate with each other, and you can receive well enough from outside telepaths that know your patterns. It shouldn't take too much to get you all to where you can send to and receive from anyone in the Alliance." Royanna explains as they all sit in Rachael's garden after the tests are complete. "With that ability alone you qualify for complete membership into the Alliance, not just for our protection of you."

"We will need to find a way to open up your minds for sending to us." Rachael informs Belina. "As Royanna has said you can receive our thoughts as long as we know your patterns, but we don't receive your thoughts. I hope that in time, with others around you, your people will learn to adjust their sending frequency when needed. After a while you won't even have to think about it."

Belina nods at everything they have told her and considers what it will mean to her people. Though they had agreed to accept membership into the Alliance before they had left Brightstar, she still wasn't sure if it was exactly right for them. They had all agreed that they couldn't go on as they had been. Their contact with others had not really given them much insight into the nature of those different from them.

"In all the time our people have moved among other races, we still have no real insight to the nature of those that are different from us."

"What about the personal plays your people do? Don't they give you some insight into what the people may be like?" Royanna asks with a slight frown of confusion. She would think that such plays would tell a lot about a people.

"Only if their within fifty to a hundred years." Shayara confirms. "Most people haven't changed much in that time period unless something significant has happened to bring about change. They will usually have the same ideas and perceptions in most cases."

"That is true Shayara. Then there are the changes that make no sense to anyone." Royanna agrees.

They sit in the garden for a while longer discussing what the Emorphas planned to do in the future and what they felt they would need in assistance from the Alliance. Though Belina tells them that they have gotten more than they ever expected. She herself would like for the troupe to have its own security team.

"Though I'm sure that nothing like what happened with the Federation will happen again. I still think that we should have that extra precaution."

"Discuss your feelings with Leyla and Thayer then Belina. I'm sure that they could set up something for you." Royanna tells her with a gentle smile. "If your people are willing, I think that we might even try introducing some of the actors and actresses from the other worlds into your troupe if you think they could work together."

Belina looks to her daughter for the answer to that. Shayara considers it for a minute. "We would have to do auditions like for anyone else, but I don't see any in the troupe disagreeing to the suggestion."

"Would their not being able to change their appearance as you do cause any problems?" Rachael asks frowning slightly.

"No, not at all. Some of our troupe don't like to take on the appearance of other people so they act as bit characters. Then there are times when it isn't even necessary to change ones appearance. Sometimes the character just needs a regular no frills look and it doesn't really matter what they look like as long as they have the basic coloring and shape." Shayara admits.

"Good, then I think that is something else you may want to consider. It could even be a way to add the security without anyone being the wiser." Royanna puts in thinking that it would solve many problems. "No one would think that the extra people were security especially if they did work on the stage. In fact I think it would be better that way. It would show that you still feel secure and that you aren't holding everyone responsible for the actions of a few people. How soon do you think it will be before you start performing again?"

Shayara frowns and looks at Pariben who has remained mostly quiet through the discussion. "I don't know, what do you think Pariben? You manage most of our performances."

"I don't think we'll do any performances until things are settled with the Federation." He tells them having considered it carefully. "We may still do some for the people that haven't joined the Federation. They were the ones we did most of our shows for any way. We didn't start doing shows within the Federation until about five or six years ago. In fact I think we've only done about thirty or forty shows throughout the Federation in all that time." He tells them going over a mental list of all the performances he had arrange in Federation space.

After a little bit longer discussion, they finally agree that they would talk it over with Leyla and Thayer after Pariben and Shayara discussed it with the rest of the troupe. They tell Royanna and Rachael that everyone is part of any decision that affects their people as a whole. If even one person disagrees with an idea then it is dropped or revised and put before the people again. Theirs was a truly democratic society. Decisions were made by the people for the people, not a select few.

That evening at a gathering of their family and friends, Salis and Colt ask that their lifemating be done within the week instead of waiting the four months. Neither of them can see the point of waiting any longer.

"Nothing will change in that amount of time, and we are closely joined already since I used my fire to heal Colt. His body accepted the fire, and in doing so has already accepted a part of me into himself."

The room becomes quiet as Salis and Thayer exchange looks. After several moments Thayer smiles and nods his agreement. "You're right sweetheart, there is no reason to wait. Do you have any reason not to join them Kasmen?"

The High Priest shakes his head solemnly and looks from Salis to Colt. "I see no reason to wait either. We can have the ceremony in four days' time, at the start of the new moon."

Everyone congratulates the couple and talk begins on the celebrations to be held after the ceremony. While the others are discussing the celebrations, Kasmen takes Salis and Colt to the side for a private conversation.

"Will you have the traditional ceremony with the royal families and your relatives present, or will you have a more private ceremony?" He asks looking from one to the other.

"What does the traditional ceremony entail Lord Kasmen?" Colt wants to know before agreeing one way or the other.

"With a traditional ceremony, the Kings and Queens, princes and princesses, and your immediate family members are present throughout the whole of your joining." He explains, then waits to see if they understand his meaning. Salis is the first to catch what he's saying and pales slightly.

"You mean they would be there for the physical joining as well?!" She asks in shock and begins to blush.

Kasmen nods. "That is what I mean Princess. Before Calidon was moved away from Manchon, all lifematings were done in such a manner. It was believed that all those who observed the lifemating, blessed the couple and strengthened their bonds. You do not have to do it this way though. You can select those that you wish to participate, or you can have no one there at all. The decision is yours and yours alone to make. Only Rachael and I remember the traditional ceremony. No one will fault you if you do not wish to follow it."

Colt and Salis look at each other and then at their family. They would like to do the traditional ceremony, but neither of them are comfortable with the idea of making love with an audience, especially one that would include their parents.

"We'll let you know what we decide tomorrow night Kasmen." Salis assures him quietly. "We need to discuss everything first." Kasmen nods his understanding and walks over to where the others are talking.

"I don't know if I could handle them watching us make love Salis. It should be private."

"Yes, I know Colt." Salis agrees looking over at Kasmen with a frown and slowly going over everything that he had said. "I don't think that they would be watching us though Colt." She says to him still watching Kasmen, then turns back to him. "He said that they would be present to observe the lifemating. The lifemating is the joining of the spiritual bodies and minds. A physical joining is merely the final expression of that spiritual joining. I believe that they will only see the spiritual not the physical. They will be a part of the spiritual to give their blessings and to strengthen our bond to each other and to them. When we go to the physical, they will still be in the spiritual aspect strengthening their own bonds of friendship and love. That's why the Majichonie and Calidonians have been so close since mother and father's joining."

Both Salis and Colt turn to look at Kasmen as he speaks to their minds. *'That is right Salis. A physical joining is the most private of all joining's and should only be known to the man, the woman, and the Great One. He is the only one who can bless that union.'*

'Why didn't you just tell us this before when you mentioned the ceremony?' Colt questions him with a mental frown.

Kasmen excuses himself from the others and rejoins them. "You had to reconcile your minds to what would happen. I knew that given time my words would become clear to you. I did tell you everything when I mentioned the ceremony, but I did not speak in a way that would give you all the information in plain view." He tries to explain. "If a traditional ceremony is to take place then it must be totally accepted in the mind. Your mind worked out all of the information and has accepted it as possible. Now it is completely your decision on how you wish to proceed. Take the next twenty-four hours to decide. Look at tapes of other lifematings and how they were held and decide which ceremony is right for you."

EPILOGUE

On the night of the new moon, the royal families join together with the Blackwoods and their mates for the lifemating of Salis and Colt. Together they create a double ring, in the center of which Salis and Colt will be joined. Their robes will be in shades of blue and gold.

Kasmen leads Salis and Colt into the Palace garden, to the center of the circles, and has them kneel on the cushions placed there. He places a hand on each of their heads before speaking. "We are gathered here on the night of the new moon to witness and bless a new lifemating. Salis and Colt wish to share this special time with you, their family and friends. Your presence here will strengthen not only their bonds, but your own bonds as well. Please join hands with those beside you now." He waits for them to do this before continuing. He nods for Christa to step forward with the lifemating goblet.

Before handing the goblet to Kasmen, Christa turns it once to the left and then twice to the right. When she finishes the last right turn she warms the contents with the pure and unconditional love she has for them both. It boils slightly, then stops and she hands it to Kasmen with a large smile. Kasmen nods his approval and signals that she should return to her place between her parents. Before doing so she smiles at Colt and Salis. Kasmen waits for her to take her place before continuing.

"This goblet contains the light of truth and the pure and unconditional love felt for this couple. It was warmed by a child that gives that love freely and with no qualifications. It is one of the strongest loves there are. Colt and Salis, please state your vows and then drink from the goblet. If your love is true, pure, and unconditional, then your spirits will join." He holds the goblet out to Colt and places it into his left hand.

"I am Colton Blackwood, born on Earth of a Majichonie male, and an Aquilian female. Conceived in love, born of love, and raised with love, I will give unto you the love to match all of these and more. You are my other half, which no other could ever be. Together we are one true love. Our love will heal all pains and sorrows and last through all of eternity and beyond." He places the goblet into his right hand and then drinks half the contents.

Kasmen takes it from him and places it into Salis' left hand.

"I am Salis Tahquor Starhawk, born on Calidon of a Calidonian man and woman. Conceived in love, born of love, raised with love and hate, reborn through the love of another Calidonian woman and a Majichonie male. I will give unto you only the love of all of these and more.

You are my other half, which no other could ever be. We are one true love that is never ending. Our love will heal all pains and sorrows and last through all eternity and beyond." She places the goblet into her right hand and drinks the other half of the contents.

Kasmen takes the goblet from her and holds it high above their heads. Together they say the last of their vows.

"All that I am I share with you. All that you are I accept unto myself as a part of myself."

Moments later the goblet begins to glow with the white light of pure love, and then leaves Kasmen's hands to float about their heads. As it gets brighter and brighter it finally bursts into a fine white powder that showers down over everyone present. Suddenly, without them thinking of it, they transform into fiery entities. Colt's transformation is a slight shock to most of those watching. Only Thayer and Christa understand the meaning of Colt becoming a fire entity. Colt is now the Fire Phoenix. He died in the flames of love and was reborn in that love.

They return to their human forms with the white glow of their spirits surrounding them. When the others see this glow, it calls to their own spirits and they too begin to glow as their spirits reach out to bless and strengthen the new couple. After receiving the blessings and strength from the others and returning the same back to them, Salis and Colt are separated from the others and their physical bodies lay down upon the cushions as their robes fall away. Their need to become physically one blocks out all thought of those around them.

They look deeply into each other's eyes before bringing their bodies together in perfect union. Their movements are slow at first and then quicken. As they reach the pinnacle of their physical love they experience what the other is feeling and seeing. They delight in their true oneness, and their ultimate sharing.

When the aftershocks of their mutual release finally fades, they realize where they are and look up and around. They are alone in the gardens, with Kasmen and Rachael standing off near the garden entrance looking the other way. As they look around, they see a double row of pure white roses. Salis cries softly into Colt's shoulder. She knew now that their union was truly blessed, for white roses had not bloomed on Calidon for nearly seventy-five years.

Merrilynda Blackwood-Nightstorm feels a small loss as she watches her twin brother's lifemating. Though she and Nightstorm are mated, theirs is not as a mating of the souls as this one is. She doesn't begrudge her twin this blessing. Nightstorm is her chosen destiny and they have been very happy since their bond mating three years ago. Though they haven't yet been blessed with a child, she would not trade her life with him for all the children in the universe. Though it would be a joy, she is convinced that when it is time they would have a child.

Rachael watches young Merri and her bond mate Nightstorm after the lifemating of her twin. She can feel their love and happiness in each other and their unuttered sorrow of not having a child. She feels deeply for their lack, but knows that it is not meant to be. When she was reintroduced to Nightstorm and they had shaken hands, she had a vision of him dying and Merri suffering a great sadness. Knowing that she could not tell of what she has seen, she gives nothing away to the couple or any of the others. It was not her place to interfere with the fates. She would grieve for them and their families, and pray to the Great One to keep Merri's grief and sorrow manageable for her mind and spirit. She will pray to Him to keep anger from poisoning her heart.

Though Merri would not carry Nightstorm's children, she would mother many children that would bring her great joy and she would honor him through one of her male children insuring that his memory and legacy would never die. All of her children would honor his memory for their mother's sake and by doing so bring honor to their family and their people for centuries to come.

A couple of weeks later, before they leave Manchon to return to Earth, Rachael meets privately with Merri and carefully implants all of her knowledge of healing and medicine into Merri's mind, along with the ability to advance that knowledge when necessary. The knowledge would come to her in stages. This knowledge would not be able to help her to save her bond mate, but in the years to come, after her mate's death, these things will bring her some comfort. She will be able to come up with cures for that which others have given up, or never come across before. She will be instrumental in saving many who would otherwise have died without her knowledge and dedication. In time she will become one of the great Master Healers on the wings of a new dawning.